ARTIFACT OF THE SKY GODS

THE DANIEL CODEX™ BOOK TWO

JUDITH BERENS   MARTHA CARR   MICHAEL ANDERLE

ARTIFACT OF THE SKY GODS TEAM

Thanks to Early Readers

Debi Sateren, Michael Robbins, Kathleen Fettig,
Terry Hicks Bennett, Bep Hvilsted-Koopman

Thanks to the JIT Readers

John Ashmore
Nicole Emens
Misty Roa
Peter Manis
James Caplan
Paul Westman
Mary Morris
Angel LaVey
Danika Fedeli

If we've missed anyone, please let us know!

Editor Lynne Stiegler

From Martha

To everyone who still believes in magic
and all the possibilities that holds.
To all the readers who make this
entire ride so much fun.
And to my son, Louie and so many wonderful friends who
remind me all the time of what
really matters and how wonderful
life can be in any given moment.

From Michael

To Family, Friends and
Those Who Love
To Read.
May We All Enjoy Grace
To Live The Life We Are
Called.

CHAPTER ONE

The late afternoon sun glinted off the Hudson River, and Daniel Winters squinted against the glare. He turned to look at the woman's corpse nestled in a copse of trees near the riverbank. She was sprawled on the ground not far from the railroad tracks, but he didn't need to be a coroner to know her injuries weren't from an impact with a train. Even a child would know she'd been murdered.

Someone or something had burned several holes through her chest. Each wound was surrounded by charred and cauterized skin at the entry and exit points. Not exactly a standard 9mm to the chest, he reflected wryly.

Not pretty, but in the end, there isn't a great way to die.

The CIA agent knew of several different weapons and types of magic that might produce such wounds, but that didn't answer the more fundamental questions that nagged at him.

Why am I here? What was Tim thinking? I have to hide that

I'm CIA and at the same time, investigate for Codex. What a twisted start to the day.

The local police had already cordoned the site off and now combed the area carefully for evidence. Police drones circled overhead and took pictures for later analysis. It didn't matter if the murder did involve magic. The police still had a job to do and would be efficient.

He was there undercover. Company spooks were never welcome in domestic cases, but despite the swarm of local authorities, he wasn't concerned. He could provide convincing FBI credentials, both physical and electronic, to anyone who asked him for identification. The subterfuge allowed him to wander the scene with impunity, but he still had no clue why his boss had sent him there.

Daniel sighed and retrieved his phone, even though he didn't need it. The custom communications device in his ear worked well, but he didn't want a bunch of local cops and CSI's to think he was talking to himself. He walked away from the main group of investigators and reached into his pocket to activate his silence cube.

Most people wouldn't notice the lack of sound if they were far enough away to not expect to hear him speak.

"Did everyone forget who I work for?" He frowned and shook his head. Even if Ronni couldn't see him, maybe he could *will* his displeasure through to her.

"Huh?" she responded. "What are you talking about? Did one of the locals question your fake credentials? They shouldn't be able to. The CIA would, but not the locals."

Daniel chuckled. "They aren't the problem. I was talking about you."

"Me?" Ronni sounded offended. "What do you mean?"

"You contacted me and said to get here ASAP because Codex is interested. You told me Tim said it was a top priority. I assumed it was an artifact recovery, but instead, it looks like a standard homicide to me. Solving those isn't high on our responsibility list unless there were some major organizational changes that no one told me about."

A small evidence drone whirred by him.

I'm already busy working for the CIA and hunting aliens for Codex. I don't have time to play detective, too, even if magic was involved. He frowned. Maybe the weapon had been a special artifact. That would explain why he'd been sent out.

"Well, I wouldn't say it was...um, standard," Ronni replied. "She wasn't strangled or stabbed or anything. You saw the body, right? Those aren't normal injuries."

Daniel sighed. "Yeah, I saw the body. So what? She was probably killed by some magical, but that's hardly breaking news. More importantly, it's not my damned responsibility unless it's part of some terrorist plot. Officially, I'm CIA, and this is US soil. I'm not a homicide detective, so I don't understand why Tim insisted you make me race out here. Even if it *were* my responsibility, it's not like I have some brilliant insight the local cops could use to crack the case."

"Oh...oh, I'm sorry. It's my fault." Ronni sighed. "I get why you're confused now."

He frowned, more bewildered than before. "*Your* fault?"

"Yeah. I double-checked some stuff while you were on the way and everything makes more sense now, although I didn't know this earlier."

He tried to keep his voice calm and reminded himself that she wouldn't deliberately mess with him.

"Care to explain? Because I don't follow you at all."

She exhaled a long, slow breath. "Okay, this is where it gets weird. The police had already identified the victim, so they went to her house to talk to her family, and…uh, she opened the door."

His frown became a scowl. "She? She who? Who opened the door?"

"The woman, or at least a woman who looked like her."

"She's got a twin? For real?" He laughed. "It'll make for an interesting movie later, I guess. I still don't see why this should involve me."

"Well…you see, the local police chalked it up to her being a twin until some alleged FBI agents showed up." The word "FBI" was pronounced in a tone of obvious discomfort.

"Alleged?" Daniel glanced over his shoulder at the significant number of field agents on site. He'd avoided them for the most part, even though he had a story ready about the involvement of a different branch if he needed it.

"I'm checking on that part. I don't really trust anyone, especially since…" Ronni's words trailed off and were replaced by the sound of typing. She never liked to talk about getting burned by the Company.

He ran his hand through his hair and tried to keep the growing frustration out of his voice. "What's wrong with the FBI investigating a murder? Unlike the CIA, that's what they're supposed to do. Why would that be suspicious? The local police must have flagged it as possibly magical, so the FBI decided to hoof it over here to save the day."

"Well, you're close. Locals did a special priority DNA test, and it came back two hours later. A local cop freaked and called the FBI. They heard his story and immediately told him to take her into custody for questioning. They made it clear that they would take point on the case."

"So, the twin killed her twin?" he asked snidely. "Sounds like the stuff Greek tragedies are made of. It's sad but not unprecedented, even if she did kill her with magic or an artifact. This definitely sounds like something the Feds and locals should handle."

Ronni remained silent for several seconds before she asked tentatively, "Do you mean that someone killing their identical twin with magical weapons is something you've run into before?"

Daniel chuckled. "Okay, I haven't encountered that per se, but there was a case once of a mother who impersonated her daughter using an artifact."

He could hear her typing again, followed by the sound of one of her toys rolling across the desktop. "What has you rattled?"

"The agents who came for the woman weren't FBI, Daniel. They were CIA."

"Way to bury the lede." He frowned and glanced at the agents again, searching for familiar faces. "Wait. If they were CIA, why were they investigating some random homicide to begin with? And why did they need me to show my face?"

"I had to go around a pretty dense firewall earlier, and the information isn't accessible to me anymore. Tim wants you there to check out the first responders, but be careful —they might be Fortis agents. The CIA agents took her to a black site after the test results came back. The thing is, she's not only a twin, but she's also a perfect genetic twin."

"So what? She's identical, right?" Daniel risked a quick

look over his shoulder again. He frowned at the FBI team and wondered if any of them were CIA agents in disguise.

"It doesn't work like that," Ronni replied. "Even identical twins have small differences in their DNA that can be detected these days. The woman at the house, though, had no differences. She was an exact match. A perfect copy." She sighed, the sound followed by more toy-rolling. "And that's not the weirdest thing about the whole situation."

He laughed. "There's more? This is downright bizarre, and I finally see why I was called out."

I think I know where this is going.

She gasped and her voice dropped to a whisper as she read from her screen, "The murder victim had no twin. When CIA showed up rather than the PDA, Tim was convinced this wasn't about a spell gone wrong. He thinks it might be extraterrestrial, and he wants you to see if you can discover anything. Fortis might be ahead of us on this one, but that doesn't mean they've won."

The CIA agent turned to look at the body as a technician took pictures with a small drone camera.

Daniel narrowed his eyes "An alien? So, if this does involve extraterrestrials, who is the alien, the victim or the murderer? Maybe even both?"

"We don't know. For now, when you finish poking around there, Tim wants you to go to the black site. Try to get information out of the woman without tipping anyone else off. He'll send you the location through the official channels in case anyone checks later."

He laughed. "Wait, you want me to go into a possible Fortis den?"

Ronni sighed. "I don't. Tim does. From what I've found out, it isn't Fortis-controlled—at least, the site where they're holding her isn't—and they don't say she's an alien. Officially, they claim she's with New Veil."

His last run-in with the anti-magic terrorists hadn't left him with any warm, fuzzy feelings for them. He might want to secure a New Veil prisoner in a black site, too.

He frowned. "And we're sure she isn't simply a terrorist? Maybe they've played around again with magic they don't understand, something that copies their bodies or crap like that."

"It's possible, but I've seen a few of those experiments, and they don't usually end well. We're honestly not sure, but Tim still wants you to look into it. I'll send you the location details. He's working on your clearance for the site, and it should be ready by the time you arrive."

The Codex phone that connected him to the brownstone buzzed a few seconds later with the information.

He scowled at the address. "Guess it's time to see if our prisoner wants to call home."

Daniel placed his thumb on the DNA scanner. A curious outsider might have wondered why a random storage unit building needed that level of security. Fortunately, the private building was tucked miles away from any neighborhood and attracted no passersby.

Nice little hidden prison. This makes the fifth one I've been read into. I wonder how many the CIA has all over the country?

He took a deep breath to regain his focus. It was time to see how well his mentor had pulled strings without drawing too much attention. After a slight burning sensation on his thumb, the door buzzed and clicked open. He stepped into a darkened hallway lit with red bulbs that he swore someone had pilfered from a World War Two submarine movie.

This place isn't as secure as it could be, but they probably plan to move her somewhere offshore soon. For all we know, if this is Fortis, maybe they have black sites over on Oriceran already.

A gorilla of an agent stood in the hallway. Daniel didn't recognize him. The man stuck out one hand and rested the other on the grip of a pistol holstered at his side. Meeting his gaze calmly, Daniel offered the guard a badge.

The gorilla ran a scanner over it and grunted. He gestured with his head toward the back of the hall. "You're slow. You better hurry before he interrogates the clone woman without you."

He? So somebody's already here, but who...and is it Fortis?

Daniel grinned. "I wonder if this raises my clearance to a new level of weird?"

The agent didn't crack a smile. Someone needed a funny-bone transplant.

He shrugged and made his way down the hall to a narrow metal door, which opened into a brightly lit room. The otherwise featureless area contained several chairs around a metal table with a small tablet on it. Through the one-way mirror, he saw the woman seated on a gray metal bench, her knees pulled to her chest. Her cell didn't even have a toilet. A small adjacent corridor led to the locked door.

Damn. She really is identical, minus the damage. Then again, it's no surprise, given that she's the same all the way down to her DNA.

Another agent stood near the window and frowned as he entered. Daniel recognized him from headquarters—Troy Williams.

Oh, it had to be this guy.

He managed to keep a smile on his face. After the incidents with Ronni and Jack Buckley, Timothy had worked on identifying possible Fortis agents. Troy Williams was near the top of that list. He also happened to be a dick, but that was incidental.

Or perhaps it wasn't. Maybe Fortis recruited a certain personality type—the kind of man or woman who could kill innocent Americans and not even blink.

Troy spared him a quick and somewhat dismissive glance. "What are you doing here, Winters?"

"The same thing as you, I imagine. I was told to look into this." Daniel shrugged. "I do what I'm told. Terrorist, artifact—whatever comes down the pipe."

The other agent snorted. "Just because you tangled with New Veil doesn't mean I need you here. It's not like you're a fucking expert after recovering some stupid portal leaves."

He still claims she's a terrorist. That might be the truth or merely his cover. Better not give him any reason to suspect me.

Troy gestured toward the tablet on the table. "That's the briefing information they sent. Don't bitch at me about the redactions. It's above my pay grade."

Daniel picked up the tablet and skimmed the document, which was all but useless. The unredacted parts didn't do much more than reiterate what Ronni had already told him after hacking into the system. It didn't make sense for the Company to redact something they passed along to agents at a black site. The one new piece of information was provided in a single cryptic line:

Informant [REDACTED] provided information that subject might be a member of a [REDACTED] group hostile to the interests of the United States.

Informant? Do they pay someone on the side to sniff out aliens?

He glanced at the woman again. In a world that included easily identifiable elves, gnomes, and pixies, the idea that someone could be an alien but look completely human was unnerving.

"We should get the interrogation started." Troy scowled and slammed a hand against the mirror. The woman leapt from the bed and rushed into a corner, trembling visibly. "But the higher-ups say they're still gathering background information. So instead, we waste fucking time while the rest of her buddies get away. Perfect."

"It's not like she's going anywhere." Daniel shrugged and tried to keep his tone conciliatory. "Come on. You know how this goes. It might take days to make any headway."

Troy sneered. "Not if we're extra-persuasive."

"And what do you mean by that?"

"You've dealt with New Veil. You know how fucked up and ruthless those guys can be." The man glared at the window and his fingers twitched at his sides like he wanted to punch through it. "We won't have a tea party with a fucking terrorist."

This guy is chomping at the damned bit to get in there. "Unless we suspect she has immediately actionable intelligence, there's no reason to question her right away."

"Don't become the pain in my ass today."

"I'm not gonna go there. Besides, it's not like you can ask her point-blank about what she really is."

Like a new kind of alien. No, that's not their play here. He looked at the terrified woman. *They may or may not suspect me, but they won't get sloppy after what happened with Buckley.*

Troy's phone buzzed, and he frowned. He pulled it out and shook his head as he stormed toward the door. "I'll be back in twenty minutes. Don't interrogate without me. I won't let you take all the credit on a case that's supposed to be mine."

"I won't. I'm not the one in a hurry."

"Whatever." The other agent threw the door open, stepped out, and slammed it shut behind him.

His case? We should both be overseas hunting artifacts or taking terrorists down, not investigating this local crap. Plus, there's no way a New Veil member would have submitted that quietly.

He pulled a chair out and sat. With a casual gesture, activated the silence cube in his pocket, confident that the tech in his subcutaneous communication device could bypass whatever interception the CIA had set up. At the minimum, they obviously hadn't hardened the facility to stop EM transmissions. This wasn't the kind of place designed to hold anyone for a long time or conduct serious

Company business. It wasn't even a good place for a proper interrogation.

Everyone's in a damned hurry. They could have simply left her at that house until they had more intel. Did they have some reason to think she'd run? What have I missed? What has Tim missed?

Daniel lowered his head to fake rereading the document. At this angle and provided he murmured, the two tiny cameras in the corner of the room wouldn't see his lips move and no one would suspect that he communicated with his remote backup support. He reached up to scratch his ear and gave it a surreptitious squeeze to activate his comms device.

"How am I supposed to interrogate a possible alien with a useless document that doesn't tell me anything I don't already know? Talk about setting me up for failure."

Ronni sighed. "That's your area of expertise, not mine."

"If I go in there and Troy finds out, he'll know something's up. Worse, if he's Fortis, that'll cause more than a little trouble. It could end up with someone dying."

"Okay, that's a problem I can help you with. Not the dying, but him knowing. Any idea how long he'll be gone?" Confidence filled Ronni's voice.

Daniel glanced at the door. "He said about twenty minutes."

"Perfect. More than enough time." She clapped, the sound sharp through the receiver. "Let's do this."

"Oh? What do you have in mind?"

"Tim sent me a file, thankfully, detailing the site's security measures. I couldn't pull this off without it. I should be able to loop the cameras for a few minutes. It'll require me to kill the power to the rest of the room, too, but anyone monitoring the footage will see you reading at the desk."

He scratched his chin. "A few minutes? That's cutting it awfully close."

"If I set it for longer, they'll know something is up. But are you sure you want to talk to this woman by yourself? She might have killed her doppelganger and taken her place." She sighed. "For all you know, she has heat vision."

Daniel snorted. "If she turns out to be an evil Kryptonian, I have a gun I can show her. I'm not kneeling to Zod."

"Kryptonian? I haven't heard of that species. Are they Oriceran? You don't think this has anything to do with aliens after all?"

He stifled a groan. "I know what to get you for Christmas this year. DC comic 104 from my personal collection."

"Huh?"

The agent sighed. "Never mind. Go ahead and do it. Time's running out."

"Okay. Give me a minute."

Daniel waited patiently and stared through the glass at the woman who now paced the length of the room. He'd dealt with countless liars, assassins, and spies who pretended to be something other than what they were, so he searched her for clues.

The fear on her face looked genuine, but that didn't mean she was what she appeared to be. Even if she was some sort of alien who'd taken the cellular structure of a murder victim, she'd been captured by hostile men in suits with bad attitudes. Plenty of professionals panicked under pressure.

Are you an alien, or is this purely some weird coincidence? If you are, did you kill that woman? Were you defending yourself?

The lights dimmed and the emergency lights kicked on. The woman in the room wrapped her arms around her shoulders and her eyes widened.

For a ruthless killer, she scares easily. She either qualifies for best actress award or something doesn't add up. I do not like puzzles.

Ronni exhaled a sigh of relief. "The outer lights are fine, and if I've read this file right, you should have five minutes before anyone realizes that something's wrong with the camera. Get to it, sir."

"*If* you've read the file—you know what? Who cares? You're right. It's time to go." Daniel stood abruptly and moved to the wrong door. "Shit. Will the DNA scanner work without power?"

"No, but the door will be unlocked for the next few minutes. It's a really poor design, actually. It needs power to maintain the lock."

"I'll tell the contractors who built the place." Daniel snorted. "That's what the Feds get for always using the lowest bidders."

Ronni laughed.

He opened the correct door and the woman spun toward him, panic on her face. "You have to help me. There's been a mistake. They don't understand what happened. I'm not what they think I am. It's…I can't…"

I wonder what percentage of murderers actually confess to their crimes straight out.

"Let's start with your name."

"Linda… Linda Hunter."

"I admire that you're sticking to the storyline." Daniel shrugged and opened his arms wide. "We have a dead woman who looks exactly like you—and, in fact, is identical right down to her DNA—and said woman didn't die of old age. You must admit that looks a little suspicious. If you're Linda Hunter, who's our body?"

The woman shook her head. "I know it looks bad, but it's…" She slipped her hand into her pocket.

Those idiots didn't check her for weapons?

He had his gun out in a blink of an eye. "Slowly."

She swallowed and inched her hand deeper. After the distinct sound of Velcro separating, she removed a small metal square with two glyphs on it. Her movements careful and slow, she held it out to him.

Between the Munich gun, the Vancouver nozzle, and some of the Codex artifacts, he recognized the alien symbols immediately.

Daniel narrowed his eyes, his gun still raised. "And what's that supposed to mean?"

"Ask Peter," she murmured. "He'll know."

"Peter? Peter who?" He already had a sinking feeling he knew the answer.

"Peter Rooney. Can you find him? Is he still alive? Tell me you can find him." She wrung her hands and waited for his answer.

Dammit straight to a freaky hell. "Yeah, I know him. He's still upright."

What the hell? The way Pops spoke, he wasn't sure what all the alien stuff meant. Now suddenly, some possibly alien woman asks for him by name?

He backed away slowly and holstered his weapon.

"Don't try anything stupid if you want to make it out of this alive. I won't promise that I can get this to him either."

"All I ask is that you try. It's important."

Daniel closed the door, stepped into the observation room, and sat at the table. "Turn the power back on, Ronni," he whispered.

The main lights flickered on. He shook his head, stood, and stomped to the door. His usual charming front had cracked a little around the edges.

He spared one last glance at the one-way mirror. The woman stared right at the glass, a mournful look on her face.

Everyone's got too many damned secrets.

Daniel kept his face blank as he approached Timothy's office in the brownstone. He was glad his mentor and the founder of their little rogue team didn't want to meet at Company headquarters. Even if they both knew how to hide their activities within the building, there was still the chance that something would get out, especially if it involved some loud yelling. An angry confrontation might tip Fortis off, and with so many eyes already on him, it would be hard to keep this a secret.

I bet those bastards watch both of us damned closely after Buckley.

Having a list of a few possible agents wasn't good enough. The other rogue team had enough power to burn Ronni and murder Jack Buckley after they'd framed him as an addict. Daniel doubted Timothy had the same resources and clout.

I'd better get this shit over with before I lose my nerve.

He took a deep breath and knocked.

"Come in," Timothy called.

The agent opened the door and stepped inside. His mentor sat behind his desk and squeezed his stress ball, the action a trademark by now.

Good thing he has that. Ronni has her toys, but comic books trump them all.

The balding, older man sighed. "Fortis has covered their tracks well. Obviously, they had to be involved in black-bagging the woman, but the trail leads to standard terrorism channels and goes cold. I still can't figure out how they knew to test her to begin with. Everything I can find points to an informant."

Daniel crossed his arms and fixed him with a hard look. "I don't want to talk about that right now."

Timothy snorted. "Is there a better time when you can pencil me into your schedule so we can talk about rogue CIA conspiracies and aliens?"

"I'm tired of people fucking lying to me, Tim," he snapped. "So, yeah, let's talk about what I want to talk about right now. I don't think that's so wrong."

The older man laughed. "Hard to work in the CIA and not deal with lies, son. I get that you've had to face some hard truths recently, but what the hell suddenly brought this attitude on?"

Daniel narrowed his eyes. "I don't have time for damned games. I need the answer to *one* fucking question. Do you know my grandfather, and did he work with you on alien shit?" Technically, that was two questions, but who the hell was counting?

Timothy frowned and shook his head slowly. "No. Hang on, don't storm out. I know *of* him, but I didn't work with him. Same thing with your parents if that's your next question. I passed the information I found about them to you as soon as I learned it."

"Maybe, but would you have done that if I wasn't on your little rogue team? You can't say that truth is your number-one priority."

"Of course not. I'm an old spook working different sides of the game. What part of that screams rigorous honesty?" The older man frowned and gave his stress ball a hard squeeze. "It's not like I want to sign my own death warrant or those of the other people around me. What the hell, Daniel? You're angry that I didn't tell you everything. Get ready to stay angry because that'll never happen. Do you tell me everything? No? I didn't think so, and yet I still manage to work with you."

Daniel shook his head. "I know you have your reasons, but this is about family. I need to know...everything. The mystery woman at the black site asked for my grandfather by name and showed me some of the same alien symbols. What made her trust me enough to do that?"

"I don't know what to tell you, son." Timothy shrugged. "She could have targeted you. She could be reading your mind. It's not like we have any real information on aliens. Come back in a minute," he yelled after a soft knock at the door. "It's my everything bagel," he explained. "Gotta eat, even in the middle of a slow alien invasion."

"Do you know if my grandfather is in the middle of this mess?"

"I don't know, and I swear that's the truth. But be careful, especially at Langley. You saw what happened to Jack Buckley. If we get sloppy, people will kill us without a second thought. Are we done? I like my bagel warm." He opened a drawer, tossed his ball inside, and slammed it shut. "I'll tell you what I think you need to know, and you'll trust me and live with that answer. That's always been the deal. But here's a freebie: I don't know why that woman asked for him."

The two men locked gazes, and Daniel's jaw clenched.

He had accepted that he couldn't lean on others, but he'd need to watch his back more carefully if he didn't want to end up dead in a shawarma restaurant.

Maybe I should take Pops' Fresca away until he cracks. Damn his pension. He'd simply buy more. He let himself slide into his easygoing role, smiled, and relaxed his shoulders. "I accept your terms, of course. We share what we can, and we trust each other as much as we can."

"The Company Hallmark card. We trust you, sort of."

Daniel sighed. "That's not the point, anyway. The live version of Linda Hunter needs help. Williams was ready to torture her for information. I'm sure he's behind the grab. If we want to help her, we'd better find a way to call the goons off before they toss her in a hole where we'll never find her. If she's an alien, innocent or otherwise, time's running out, Tim."

His companion sucked in a deep breath. "Okay. I'll work on that. But I need you to keep your head in the game. Things could get messy if and when we make our move."

"Don't worry about me. I have this all under control." He opened the door.

"Daniel," his mentor called.

He looked over his shoulder. "What?"

"I'm not lying about your grandfather."

I really wish I could believe that, Tim. "Enjoy your bagel."

CHAPTER TWO

The next morning, the CIA agent stood at the front counter of his shop, Rooney's Antiquities and Oddities, and stifled a yawn. He'd been busy the last few days, even before Tim sent him to investigate the weird twin or clone case. His restlessness also didn't help. Several times, he'd held back from confronting Pops to demand the truth.

Linda Hunter hadn't asked for Tim, after all, but Peter Rooney. *I need to play this smart. Otherwise, I risk not learning the actual damned truth.*

He lifted a gold chain from a shelf and dusted it. When connected to a family pocket watch, it passed along any memories stored inside the timepiece. *Everyone has a piece of a damned codex. I'm working a puzzle, and it feels like I have only the blue sky segments.*

Tommy stepped through the front door with a treasure in his hand—the Green Lantern mug filled with Stumptown coffee from Killer ESP. The half-elf set the mug on the counter and grinned. Daniel was pleased to see he had no limp or any sign of pain.

It's good to have a straight-forward victory against regular goons.

"My man!" He looked at the chain, suddenly thoughtful. It would make a good Christmas gift for the boy.

A few bruises still lingered on Tommy's face, but the other evidence of his recent savage beating by the Steel Wolves gang had vanished.

"Look what I can do!" The half-elf twirled neatly on one leg and grinned again.

Daniel slipped the chain into his pocket and smiled as he remembered decimating the last of the would-be invaders. *I warned the assholes they should back off.*

"About time," he muttered and gestured with the coffee to make his point.

He fished some money out, handed it to Tommy, and tilted the large green-and-black mug to gulp the contents. It was the most efficient way he could think of to get the caffeine without injecting it directly. "I need a bigger mug."

"Dude, that holds sixteen ounces."

"Maybe someone already makes a caffeine auto-injector that would send it directly to my brain. Okay, maybe that's a bit much."

"And they call me the dreamer."

"Dreams are good. Coffee jumpstarts mine." He tilted the cup again to get the last few drops.

Tommy snorted and shrugged. "Sorry it took so long. There was a huge line."

Daniel chuckled and his fantasies of mainlining coffee vanished. "It's okay. I'm tired and grouchy, that's all. I'm useless without my caffeine."

Peter made his way down the stairs from the apartment

and into the shop. He wore baggy, green khakis that had seen better days with a belt and a short-sleeved button-down shirt. Tufts of his thick silver hair stuck up on the top of his head. "My Pop-Tarts. It's a travesty. A heinous crime."

"Morning, Pops." The agent set the mug down and smiled at his grandfather. "Yes, Pop-Tarts are a travesty and a crime against my taste buds."

"Except for the cinnamon ones." Tommy smiled despite the old man's glare.

Pops shook his head. "Those are my nighttime snacks, and they're gone. I need something easy to eat when I wake up. They're perfect—taste fine without being cooked. It's not like I want to make a sandwich in the middle of the night." He shrugged and muttered under his breath as he headed to the back room. "Sad state of affairs when a man can't have a few crumbs to himself…"

"You're playing with old-man fire, kid—the worst kind. He may be slow, but he's patient. Better sleep with one eye open," Daniel warned him.

Tommy's dad had hit the road with his band again in search of the big break, and the half-elf had stayed with them since he left.

He shrugged. "Sometimes I get hungry in the night. I'm a growing boy. Mr. Rooney looks pretty healthy, and I need the calories more."

The agent laughed. "You ate all his Pop-Tarts. I'm telling you that's a dangerous move."

"They're pretty delicious, dude. My dad never buys stuff like that. He's kind of a health nut in a lot of ways."

Daniel sighed and rolled his eyes. The teen's father was

not his favorite subject conversation. "At least you didn't go for the Fresca. We would have a full-blown riot, then. Pops would probably go find some lightning-tossing artifact for revenge."

"That might be worth it."

He gave the teen a gentle shove. "Not funny. Try to keep your hands and mouth to yourself. Pop's a good man until you take his snacks and drinks away."

"Sure thing, dude." Tommy grinned and headed toward the comics' room in the back.

"Stop," Daniel commanded.

He complied and turned to face him. "Need something?"

The agent shook his head. "No, but you do. You have places to be right about now." He nodded at a backpack which lay in front of the counter. "Go to school. You'll miss it when it's no longer free."

The teen groaned. "I doubt that."

"Doesn't matter. While you stay with me, the least I can do is make sure you go to school."

"But the Dark Avengers—"

Daniel grabbed his chest and his eyes widened. "This is a DC comics household."

"Yeah, about that… I added a few to your collection. You'll miss them when I'm grown and gone."

"You've hidden them among Batman, haven't you?"

Tommy snorted and cast one last longing look toward the back before he sighed and stepped out the front door.

Fifteen minutes later, Daniel grabbed his bag and set off for the Metro. People smiled as they walked up and down the street. Their faces reflected no tension and no evidence remained of the vicious gang that had tried to move into the neighborhood not too long ago.

This is how it works. Get rid of the crap making trouble, and people will instantly stop worrying.

He shook his head. No pity lingered in his heart for the men he'd had to kill.

The Steel Wolves might have been the first to poke their nose into Old Town, but they wouldn't be the last. *I have to be ready for them.*

The agent scanned the street for any unfamiliar people, vehicles, or suspicious drones. Nothing stood out, but that didn't mean there wasn't a threat.

A large, blue straw hat shaded the familiar face of Mrs. Carmichael as she walked down the sidewalk. She smiled, waved, and made her way to him.

"Good morning, ma'am," Daniel said with a polite nod.

"It is a good morning. How is your grandfather?"

"Same as always. Feisty and opinionated."

The woman laughed. "Better to be feisty than boring. That's what I always say." She looked around for a moment and leaned in to whisper, "I heard about what you did, you know. I'm surprised you didn't tell everyone about it. It's not like people will be mad considering who it was."

Daniel blinked, and his heart rate kicked up. Unless his world had turned completely insane, this nice, church-going little old lady couldn't possibly know that he'd walked into a savage battle in a gang hideout. Then again, his life had thrown him a lot of surprises recently. For all he knew, Mrs. Carmichael was the queen of all aliens.

"You did? What did you hear, exactly?"

She nodded gravely. "Yes, sir. Jeanine told me all about it."

"Jeanine?" Relief flooded him. She had referred to the mugging, not his attack on the gang.

The old lady crossed her arms over her ample bosom. "You and your little Dragon Dungeon poker friends stopped those muggers. You didn't even need guns to do it. That's because you're veterans, I bet."

Daniel laughed. "Dungeons and Dragons."

"That's what I said."

"Exactly. We have to look after each other." He shrugged. "That's the way to keep this a great place to live."

"Um hmm. Indeed." Mrs. Carmichael adjusted the angle of her wide-brimmed hat. "If you'll excuse me, I have a hair appointment I'd best be sure I keep. Thank you, Mr. Mayor."

"I'm not really the mayor."

The woman waved her hand dismissively as she walked away.

The agent adjusted his backpack and headed along the familiar route. Halfway to the Metro, he passed Lox and Key, a local bagel place. His stomach rumbled, and he gave in to the urge and entered the shop. He wasn't in a major hurry that morning so might as well take care of breakfast.

Daniel made his way to the counter. A few people sat at tables here and there, but he'd arrived after the morning rush.

The owner smiled in greeting. Simon was a gregarious

man with a bushy beard and neatly trimmed hair. "Daniel, it's been a while. I began to think either I or maybe a bagel had done something to offend you."

He shrugged. "I've had a weird schedule lately."

"Your usual?"

He nodded.

"One toasted raisin bagel, light on the cream cheese, coming right up." Simon took a bagel from under the counter. He sliced it in half and placed it in the toaster oven. "I feel pretty lucky, even if you haven't graced me with your presence." He set the oven timer.

The agent laughed. "Oh?"

"I heard from Charlie about how that thug came in and tried to shake him down." He smirked. "Stupid punk got what was coming to him. Cockroaches, all of them."

"How's business?"

"Never better. Everyone likes bagels, no matter which day of the week. How are things at Rooney's Oddities?"

"And Antiquities."

"Sure, sure. Old weird stuff." He held up his hands. "Because new and weird is junk."

Daniel laughed. "These days, a lot of people want a little magic."

"Sure, sure. You think that gang will come back? Maybe to bust up more shops?"

The agent managed not to snort. *They'd need a necromancer to come back at this point.*

He shook his head. "The police said they were afraid of another gang from their old territory and so left the area."

Simon shook his head. "Fear only brings you more fear.

Coffee? why am I even asking? The bagel's an excuse to get more java."

"You do know me. It's touching."

"Meh, I get it. It's good coffee." The oven beeped, and Simon removed the toasted halves. With deft movements, he applied a light coating of cream cheese. "Hey, you hear about the potluck? You coming? I'll bring scones."

"I'll tell Pops. He can bring Fresca, as usual."

Simon chuckled, wrapped the bagel in wax paper, and slipped it and a napkin into a brown paper bag. "Knowing him, he'll stand near the table and make sure no one actually takes them."

"He has issues. I'll bring enough soda to make it a non-issue. Great idea on the potluck."

"Have to send the world a message. We hang together."

"Yeah. Yeah, we do, no matter what." Daniel accepted the small bag and the coffee and swiped his phone over the payment terminal. "Have a nice day, Simon."

"That's my plan every day."

With a quick nod at the man, he left and took a bite of his bagel before he reached the metro where a nibble could get you a ticket. The raisins were warm, just the way he liked them.

Daniel took another bite and chewed thoughtfully as he studied his surroundings. This little corner of the world was supposed to be his peaceful retreat, but it had attracted notice.

There's no such thing as a safe haven unless you create one and keep it that way.

He'd be ready for the next gang that tried to move in on Old Town.

Daniel grunted as he pushed the bar above his chest. The Company gym offered every machine imaginable, including some he was sure involved weird magic that Ronni would love.

"Morning, Daniel. Trying to keep up with the teenagers?" Donald Emerson stopped beside him and glanced at two younger agents.

Daniel ignored the dig and raised the bar again. Donald eyed a machine with ropes and pullies and scratched his head hesitantly. "I want to try it, but…"

"Nessie must have put that one there. The Company probably tests a few things on unsuspecting employees."

"I suspect everyone at all times." Donald smirked and pulled on one of the handles. He leaned in and strained hard. "Son of a bitch!"

Daniel grunted in mid-lift and fought back a laugh. "Something wrong?"

"What's wrong with a good run in a pair of Converse? Newfangled junk won't last a week." The agent marched off, still muttering under his breath, and glared at the two younger agents.

Both were in their early twenties and had probably been recruited straight out of college. They shook their heads and grunted with exertion.

"Experience and skills trump brute force every time." Daniel focused on his bar again. At thirty, he was decades younger than people like Timothy, but he wasn't the fresh-faced teen who'd joined the Marines either.

He replaced the bar in the rack and slipped out from

under it to grab a few more weights. Now, he'd bench five more pounds than them.

The agent slipped back into position, took a deep breath, and lifted. His arms and chest strained with each motion.

The silent contest was his secret. All that mattered was that he knew he could match them.

Experience, skills, and brute force. He still had it.

CHAPTER THREE

The five friends leaned over their character sheets at the wooden table in Daniel's apartment. The dice lay in front of Taylor. They played the game old-school with no new tech or magical items. Rule number one was no oddities from the shop downstairs.

Connor picked up his Joe Blow—Fresca mixed with vodka—and sipped it with a glum look on his face. "Since you marauding adventurers have ruthlessly assassinated the Drow Queen, I think we should stop for tonight, gentlemen and lady."

Juan grinned. "Since when is Lorelai a lad—"

"A gentleman doesn't talk about a lady that way." Lorelai stomped on his foot.

He grimaced. "Ow, especially a dangerous one."

Daniel chuckled and savored the chocolate flavor of another Ho Ho. A favorite of his mother's, they were his game night treats two times a month.

He washed it down with a gulp of the beer he'd barely

touched. Everyone took the game seriously and he needed a clear head to win.

Taylor nodded. "I'll level up soon. We've breezed through this undercity, Connor. Why don't you put up a real fight?"

The DM shrugged. "First, the game is about mutual fun and respect. Second, your dice are ridiculous. Seriously, it's like you come to the game with the most lateral solution to all possible problems predetermined."

Daniel raised his beer with a smile. "Nothing wrong with smart players."

"I'll throw elder dragons at you," Connor muttered. "We'll see how smart you are then."

Juan finished his beer and sighed in contentment. "You know what we haven't done in a while?"

Daniel asked, "What?"

"For Want of a Dollar." Juan pulled his wallet out. "Come on. We should play a round or two."

They each added their bills to the pot.

"What's the challenge?" Daniel waved a dollar and slapped it on the table. The figurines bounced and one fell. "I have a definite advantage against you lightweights."

Juan leaned forward on his elbows. "I'll go first. Atlas is releasing pumpkin spice condoms this year in response to customer demand. True story. They'll be in your local CVS, but twenty bucks for a box of ten is a little pricey."

Lorelai guffawed. "I suppose that's to keep the ladies happy."

"Pricey? What do you buy and how many mini-Juan's will show up someday?"

"You are a sick little man, Juan."

"Do you search for this stuff on your work computer?"

Juan slapped the table. "Come on! You know how this works. Put your dollars in and declare." He sat back, crossed his arms, and challenged the others with a bold look.

"You have issues, man. Okay, I say it's real." Connor looked at Daniel.

"Why not? There's pumpkin spice everything else. Seems like an easy one."

"True! All true." Taylor leaned forward expectantly.

"You want it to be true..." Juan smirked

"Also true!"

"Total bullshit." Lorelai gave them a cool smile. "There are limits."

"Final answers?" Juan grinned. "Lorelai keeps her money." He snatched the other three dollars.

"I live another day," she declared and kissed her dollar.

Connor shrugged. "You got lucky."

She flashed him a grin. "When we did this last month, a certain someone doubled down, then tripled down, and walked out owing a dollar."

"I was tapped out," Connor grumbled.

Juan laughed. "You're not exactly paid peanuts. We all have basically the same job, so we know what you earn."

"Just saying, is all." Connor smirked. "Doesn't matter. I'll win next time."

Daniel chuckled and shook his head. The lighthearted banter eased the work tension.

I never want to lose this, no matter how far down the alien-hunting rabbit hole I go.

Juan glanced at the window. "Too bad there are no muggers. I could use the exercise."

Daniel raised a brow. "Huh? You want thugs in our neighborhood?"

The other man waved a hand. "No, no, but my fist is itching. We could bet on how many asses we kicked, or how many punches were needed. Shake things up a little."

Lorelai snorted. "From what I remember, you had your ass kicked."

Taylor laughed and thumped Juan on the back.

"Hey, to distract an enemy and tire them out so they can be flanked is a time-honored military strategy," he retorted. "I'm a fucking military genius. Just call me Juan Tzu."

Another round of laughter followed.

Taylor looked thoughtful. "It felt good. I don't know about the rest of you, but locked in a basement room reading, typing, and analyzing all day…" He shrugged. "I get it. I was Air Force intel before the civilian life. Other branches mocked us, even our own non-intel guys, and I know intelligence is important to protect the country. But sometimes, I want to punch a bad guy when he screws with someone. It's very satisfying."

He looked at Daniel and winced. "Not that I look down on you for leaving the field entirely."

"Yeah, someone has to sell stuff."

"Nice save, Connor."

If only you knew…

Daniel chuckled and shrugged. "I'm fine with my life."

Connor downed the last of his Joe Blow and shook his head. "Pounding scumbags is one thing, but I still have some cool shit with the day job. There's an opportunity coming up, and it's…out of this world."

"Why did you wink? Don't. It's not a good look." Lorelai wrinkled her nose.

Taylor frowned. "Should you even hint about something classified?"

Juan laughed. "Don't worry, man. It's no big deal. He's excited because they're sending him to Oriceran. It's not unusual these days—a free wonderland vacation courtesy of the taxpayer."

Lorelai smirked. "I'd do a Go Fund Me if they planned to send Connor into space."

"Try not to trip while out there saving the world," Juan interjected

Connor flipped him off. "Say hello to my little pumpkin spice friend."

Daniel laughed and hid his surprise. His friends were still in government intelligence jobs and could investigate Ragnarok or Nephilim.

He frowned.

Is it paranoia now? It's not like everyone is involved in this crap. Buckley was a CIA field agent, not some backlines analyst. But Ronni's not a field agent either.

He managed not to wince and forced a smile instead. There were all kinds of aliens on Earth these days. Some of them were even a new kind of normal.

Daniel sipped his coffee as he headed toward the Metro station. It was too damned early and the sun had barely poked above the horizon. Tommy had stayed the night again, so he'd sent the boy out on a pre-dawn coffee run.

He stepped into the station and through the turnstile after he'd swiped his phone over the reader.

His stomach tightened, and he turned slowly to search the crowd. A few bored businessmen stared at their phones. A high-schooler leaned against a nearby pillar and bobbed his head to the music in his huge headphones.

I'm paranoid and see Fortis in every shadow. It's like I'm a newbie waiting for a terrorist attack.

Daniel snorted. He should have gone to bed earlier.

His train arrived, and he dropped his cup into the trash before boarding. Unlike most days, he wouldn't use the Jaguar today. Even with the nanopaint camouflage capabilities, driving the flashy car too near the brownstone could attract suspicion.

The rogue headquarters was close enough to the subway station that commuting there by train was a practical part-time solution.

Does it count as paranoia if others warn you?

He chuckled, shook his head, and found a seat as the train pulled out.

Minutes later, the hairs on the back of his neck prickled with the instinct that had saved him more than one occasion.

Daniel recognized the businessmen and the high school kid. A few other passengers had boarded, including a tired-looking woman with bags and a stroller. None of them paid attention to him.

The agent tapped the camera on his phone and flipped

it. He chuckled as if at some joke and shifted slightly. No one used his apparent distraction to stare at him.

No, screw this. It can't be fucking paranoia. It's what has kept me alive. I've spent enough years in the CIA to know when I'm being watched, but where and how?

Person-to-person surveillance would be the best choice, but he couldn't rule out surveillance cameras, tiny drones, or even magic. A smart operative assumed the enemy had superior capability, and Daniel was way above the average CIA agent. He'd learned to expect anything and everything.

If they are using magic, I might not be able to pinpoint it.

He disembarked at the first stop possible. The unease remained, even once he'd boarded the next train. He no longer bothered to feign a smile. His frown would simply blend with many other commuters around him.

Should I avoid the brownstone? Maybe I should contact them.

He grabbed a pole near the doors as all the seats were already taken.

"Excuse me." A large man pushed past him and planted himself in the center of the aisle.

Daniel scowled and released a slow breath.

The doors hissed closed, and the sense of caution vanished. He peered out the window but no one lingered on the platform.

Maybe he was paranoid after all.

***

Daniel sat in the operations room and manipulated a holographic globe display with his phone. "The aerial displays aren't practical," Big Gnome said from behind him.

Ronni nodded across the table. "Interfacing the systems with custom secure apps and portable keyboards is far easier."

"Yeah, and it gets Nessie and Timothy off our backs about too much time spent 'playing around' instead of on critical infrastructure development." The gnome's phone buzzed, and he grumbled as he left the room.

"Nessie must need him."

"Good bet." Ronni pointed to a flashing triangle above Egypt. "I tried to dig deeper into that area as Fortis is very interested. From what I can tell, it seems they've sent multiple teams to investigate pyramids."

Daniel rubbed his chin thoughtfully. "Thirty years ago, the crazies said the pyramids were all made by aliens, and we laughed them off. Then we discovered they were made by Atlanteans from Oriceran, and we still scoffed. Are you now suggesting the original crazies were right?"

She shrugged. "Well, not completely. I'm sure the major pyramids were made by the Atlanteans for energy collection, but others might be connected to aliens not from Oriceran."

He leaned back and crossed his arms. "Okay, but I doubt Egypt's the only place where aliens have popped up. Lore and sightings exist all over the world, both modern and ancient. The real question is what their plan is."

Ronni cleared her throat and tapped on her keyboard. The globe disappeared and was replaced by excerpts from several documents. "It's difficult to track Fortis down, but finding information on Ragnarok and Nephilim is easier, believe it or not. DoD, Homeland Security, and even DoE money is involved. Nephilim seems far more focused on decoding the alien symbols. Ragnarok seems more interested in intent and reverse engineering."

Daniel nodded. "They want to be ready if the aliens make a big play. Does Fortis pull their strings?"

She shrugged. "I'm not sure. They receive a lot of CIA money, but their level of security is far lower than I'd expect, and they have very few alien artifacts, even compared to our rogue group."

"They're compartmentalizing. If someone stumbles onto the projects, they won't learn the government response status or the kind of things they've done." Daniel frowned as he remembered the small town that Fortis had destroyed to hide the existence of aliens. "Fortis obviously has its hands on some big toys."

Ronni typed again and the documents disappeared, replaced now by holographic projections of dozens of different artifacts. Some looked old and weathered like conventional archaeological treasures, but a few suggested advanced modern technology.

"I've tried to figure out what artifacts they have, but it's difficult because there's also no indication which are magical versus possibly alien." She sighed. "They've kept most information off the net, the dark web, and even the magicals' dark web, but there are several dangerous weapons unaccounted for that I was able to correlate with CIA activity."

Daniel snorted. *Unaccounted for like that gun I grabbed in Munich?*

"It makes sense to concentrate on weapons if they're

worried about aliens invading. More toys will hopefully mean it won't be a one-sided curb-stomp."

"I guess, but it's weird. I don't think it's only about defense. I've found a few things with Raganarok that aren't alien-focused. Instead, they're looking into how to apply alien tech against magic."

Daniel shrugged. "Plenty of groups try to mix technology and magic."

"No, this is weirder. It's not a matter of mixing magic and tech but more like directly countering magic."

"Two for one." The CIA agent reached for a Bella Swan figurine, but Ronni slid it away without looking up.

"Don't touch what you don't understand or doesn't belong to you."

"Good life rules in general."

"Particularly for agents."

"Smart plan on their part," he said as he refocused. "Develop everything you need to deal with aliens and also an uppity elf or two." He shook his head. "We don't have time to concentrate on anything but the alien angle. I doubt Fortis wants a war with Oriceran anytime soon. What else have you found out?"

She sighed. "That's the problem. Look, I need to be honest."

"About?"

She stretched her arms over her head and her neck cracked. "My limits. I'm good with computers, but my primary background is engineering, not hacking or cracking. I got burned because I wasn't careful enough. I'm a good backup, but we need a good, solid hacker, someone to access hidden Fortis servers and never get caught. That's not me."

Daniel stared at her for a moment, unsure whether this was modesty, fear, or a frank admission of her skill limitations. He decided that she wanted to do what was best for the group.

"Okay. Fair enough. Do you know anyone?"

Ronni swallowed and nodded. Several seconds passed before she spoke again. "Okay, I got a guy. Paul Slatterly."

"Paul Slatterly?" Daniel echoed. The name sounded vaguely familiar and he tried to place the man's face.

"He's not like me. He has a total information warfare background and likes gadgets but is not a tinkerer." She sighed and rubbed her palms together. "I feel kind of guilty suggesting him."

Daniel arched a brow. "Why?"

"This is so dangerous. When they killed Agent Buckley, I realized I was lucky. Anyone involved with this risks their lives." Ronni shrugged. "You're a field agent, so you're used to getting shot at by terrorists or being the target of fireballs or stabbed or blown up—"

"I get it. You don't want death as part of your job description."

"Us desk types aren't used to it."

"What about Paul? Do you think he's up for saving a few worlds?"

"Sort of." She waggled her hand in a nervous gesture. "He's kind of…um, I don't know the right word. Arrogant? He's a do-the-right-thing-no-matter what kind of guy but doesn't think the CIA is on the same track."

"He thinks we play too far inside the lines? Wow, that's a bold statement."

"Weird times and the Company prevent him truly using his talent."

"He's that talented? I won't force anyone but also won't ignore a useful resource." Daniel released a sharp breath. "Battles can be won or lost based on intelligence, and we need to get serious. Buckley proved that. The other team won't sit there and worry about danger."

She retrieved a small, blue-haired troll that blinked at him.

Daniel's eyes widened. "Holy shit! You actually brought a troll in here? Are you bonded with him? We can't keep that kind of magical under control easily. I've heard stories about food budgets alone. The last thing we need is to draw attention."

"What?" She looked at her hand. "No, no, no. It's not *that* kind of troll. It's a doll—one of my toys. I enhanced it." She tossed it to him.

He caught it and plastered a smile on his face to cover his embarrassment. The doll opened its eyes and blinked again. "Why are you giving me this?

"Paul's the best around. If you want him to seriously consider joining us, take him that. He'll know what do with it." Her face grew scarlet.

Daniel nodded slowly. Whatever Ronni hadn't said seemed more about embarrassment than deception. He had no reason to press her on it.

"You're sure? Because if I approach him and he turns us down, we'll have to wipe his memory with drugs, at a minimum. That would alert others that something happened to him."

Ronni shook her head. "I guarantee that if you explain what we do and that we need his help and uh…that I'm involved, he'll be on board."

"Okay, time to go recruit us a legit hacker. First, though, I need to grab a little something."

She slid a drawer open and rummaged around inside. "Oh, you might not need these, but after what happened to me, you might find them helpful. Take them with you so I can sleep."

"Show me what you've got."

CHAPTER FOUR

Daniel stepped off the elevator wearing his nicest default smile. This entire floor at Langley contained row after row of cubicles under a dropped ceiling with fluorescent lighting. Support staff tapped and clicked furiously on various devices.

He hadn't been there in a few months. A field agent rarely visited any of the research floors that didn't involve gadgets.

If he needed an excuse, he would tell whoever asked that Nessie wanted him to check on something. She was ready to back that up. He moved down the rows of cubicles, his neck muscles tense.

Ronni had given him a few toys, including gadgets that could conceal him from most cameras. Some even provided a way to beat the DNA scanners. But she'd also warned him that once used, they'd probably be useless by the next day once the CIA tightened their security. Nessie's updates would help her to stay current with Company upgrades.

Better save them for when I need them.

A laugh bubbled within, then faded abruptly. He had mastered a Headquarters persona and usually didn't worry about Company politics. A necessary part of the job was to form alliances with other staff members. But with every step, he now wondered if Fortis watched and waited for him to screw up.

I have a bad case of creeping paranoia.

Daniel smirked. He'd end up frazzled and unshaved like Buckley at this rate.

But unlike Buckley, he had a support group. Timothy, Nessie, and Ronni. The guys in the garage. Hell, even Madge and Big Gnome. Daniel didn't have to take on a rogue CIA conspiracy by himself.

He walked down the aisle between the cubicles, noting details along the way. He grinned and looked around. None of the desk jockeys there paid him any attention at all.

Only worried about the job, huh? That's the way to do it.

Loud clacking and a steady whirring noise emanated from beyond a cluster of several empty cubicles. The empty area formed a circular dead zone around the source of the noise—Paul's cubicle.

Daniel paused, a little startled. Multiple fans of different sizes were tacked up around the cubicle, all pointing out.

"Ugh. They call *that* a server? It's an insult to me." Paul adjusted his glasses and ran a hand through his thinning dark hair.

The agent looked at the man's desk. It was carefully arranged with everything in a tray or container and not even a single stray pen or paperclip in sight. The balding man sat in his chair and hunched over four different keyboards. Four linked monitors were spread out in front of him at different angles.

"What's with the four keyboards?"

Paul didn't answer. Maybe not the best start but not the worst either.

His fingers danced as he muttered to himself without so much as a glance at his visitor. Daniel didn't even try to follow what he was doing. He was distracted by the man's head which swung back and forth as he jerked his hands from keyboard to keyboard.

The agent cleared his throat, but Paul continued to ignore him—or maybe he hadn't even noticed him. It was hard to be sure.

"Hello, Paul."

The hacker tapped away for a few more seconds. "They are so ridiculous sometimes." He stopped and looked at Daniel with a frown. "Who are you?"

He blinked several times and pulled a stick of gum from a side pocket halfway down his cargo pants but didn't pop it in his mouth. Instead, he placed it on his desk.

"Daniel Winters. I'm a field agent."

Paul nodded, his brow furrowed. "Good for you, then."

Daniel cleared his throat again. "I'm here to talk to you about an…opportunity." He activated a Ninja Turtle anti-surveillance toy in his pocket that he'd "borrowed" from Timothy's office.

"An opportunity? What opportunity? I don't know you. If you want me tasked as backup or something, talk to my boss and fill out a form. I don't do anything without a signed form." He unwrapped the gum carefully and popped it into his mouth. "Go the hell away. I have work to do. Plenty of it. Get out of my zone area." He waved his arm, indicating all the empty cubicles.

The agent reached into his jacket pocket, pulled out the troll doll, and tossed it onto the desk.

"Hey, you don't throw—" The man's eyes widened, and he looked sharply at his visitor. "Where the hell did you get this?"

Daniel leaned forward with a cool smile. "You know where, and you know *who*. She told me that if I gave you the troll, you'd listen to my proposal."

Paul leaned back in his chair and patted the top of his head gently. "One, two, three…" He breathed out noisily. "Okay, got it. She's okay, got it." He looked at Daniel. "I tried to make contact with her after she was burned, but it was like she dropped off the face of the earth. At first, I was a little concerned she was in the ground—you know, black-bagged. Worse than six feet under." He sighed and shook his head.

"She's okay. She's lying low for a while until all this crap sorts itself out."

"Does the Company know that? Never mind, don't tell me. You know, I've been worried. I mean, I knew she wasn't dead, but I was still worried."

Daniel eyed the hacker. "How did you know she wasn't dead?"

"I found some code online recently. It…had *her* fingerprints all over it."

He nodded, both impressed and concerned at the same time.

Maybe it's a good thing we're bringing him on if he's that good.

The hacker stared longingly at the doll, and Daniel arched a brow.

"You're into her." He watched the reaction.

"One, two, three." Paul blew out another breath of air.

There's a backstory there, but it's for another time.

Daniel shot him a charming smile. "Ronni is involved with something that needs your skill set. Come to the Three Kingdoms in Chinatown tonight at eight. I'll pay. Unless you hate Chinese food."

Paul studied him cautiously. "I like Chinese food."

Daniel nodded. "See you tonight, then. I'll tell Ronni hello for you."

"One, two, three…"

The operative sipped his tea as Paul devoured a few more dumplings. He'd brought the troll doll and set it on the table. The eyes blinked disconcertingly at Daniel.

His companion looked up from his plate and spoke with his mouth full. "I'll talk when I'm done." He patted his slight paunch and looked at the remaining dumplings. "I'm not done yet."

"I'm not in a hurry."

Paul shoved the remaining dumplings in his mouth and chewed with two fingers pressed against his lips to keep it all inside. He swallowed hard. "What do you need me for?"

He moved the silence cube to the center of the table. "We're not at headquarters, but you don't want anyone to overhear us. You need an off-the-books favor. The only time one of your kind needs that is because it's not all aboveboard."

Daniel rubbed his chin. "I work for the CIA. Very little I do is aboveboard. It's probably the same for you."

The hacker licked his fingers. "Fair enough."

"I don't feel like dancing around the truth, so I'll give it to you straight, Paul."

"Fine by me." He shrugged and shoved his plate aside.

"Aliens are real."

"Yeah, so? There are elves and gnomes and crap from fantasyland. Big deal. Do you still struggle to adjust to that after all these years?" Paul smirked. "Don't feel bad. A lot of people do." A scowl crossed his face. "You're not one of those Humans First types, are you?"

Daniel shook his head. "No. I've run into that rough bunch, but I'm talking about a different kind of alien. The extraterrestrial kind from who knows where. The kind that may very well be little gray men from Zeta Reticuli. We don't know the details yet." He narrowed his eyes and wondered how far he could go with Paul. All in, apparently. "It doesn't help that the CIA has a rogue team called Fortis to assassinate CIA agents, burn CIA support personnel, and kill American citizens to bury the truth."

Paul burst out laughing and pointed his finger at Daniel. "Oh, I get it. I totally get it. See, this is why I have the fucking zone. This a field agent's punk-the-support-staff thing—a bet, or dare, or other garbage like that."

"Do you think I'd have one of Ronni toys if I were here to trick you?"

The hacker's smile froze, and he glanced at the troll. "Wait, you're serious?"

Daniel nodded. "As serious as Ronni getting burned."

He took a deep breath. "One, two, three." He exhaled hard. "I knew it… The minute they said we shouldn't believe in aliens, I knew it. If Oriceran exists, others do too." He drummed his fingers on the table. "What's the endgame of exposing the truth?"

"Making sure the planet stays relatively intact."

"Simple, direct, probably doable."

"Ronni says you're the best at getting around firewalls."

"Hell, that's pretty simple. You don't need me for that. I find the places you don't know to look for. That's where the real information lies. Info is power, and way better than money."

"Right now, the Company wants to eradicate anything to do with more aliens—and anyone trying to find out more."

"Like Ronni. You had something to do with that, didn't you? Lie to me, and we never speak again."

"She was researching something for me. I didn't know they were watching so closely. My mistake."

"So you're a dangerous guy to be around. How do you plan to find what you need and not get everyone burned—or killed?"

Daniel grinned. "Another rogue CIA team."

Paul's eyebrows shot up. "You have balls. I'll give you that. What kind of team are you?" He looked at the empty plate, then around the restaurant.

The agent waved to the waitress. "The kind that's more interested in preventing wars between any worlds."

The woman came over and waited for their order. "One more plate of dumplings, please."

He waited until they were alone. It paid to be cautious, especially now. For the right price, everyone would betray anyone. "We know very little about the aliens, and we don't think Fortis does either, but they kill first and ask questions later—like Jack Buckley."

"Jack Buckley?" Paul glanced over his shoulder, then looked at Daniel with wide eyes. "I thought he was a junkie or something who OD'd."

"Official bullshit." Daniel shook his head. "He stumbled onto the truth, and *they* took him out. Maybe Fortis, or maybe someone working for them. The point is, they killed a man for learning the truth. There has to be a better way, and we want to find it."

Paul snorted. "And why should I trust your rogue CIA team over *their* rogue CIA team?"

"Honestly?"

"Yeah, honestly."

"Because mine's got Ronni on it."

"You made it necessary. Fine, fine. One, two, three." He exhaled as the dumplings arrived, and he closed his eyes and smiled as he inhaled the aroma. "She doesn't do anything she doesn't want to do, that's for sure. Keep going. I'm still listening."

Daniel managed a smile. He knew when things were falling his way. That instinct kept him alive. "Ronni got burned because she's good but not good enough to hide her tracks from someone better. Fortis obviously has people who *are* that good, and we need to counter that." He pointed at Paul. "We need you."

The hacker took a deep breath. "Save Ronni, save the world."

"Something like that."

"Sounds like I'm the hero in this story."

"Okay, sure, you're the hero." Daniel forked a dumpling cautiously. He ignored the grunted protest from his companion. "Ronni believes you can cover your tracks, which is good enough for me." He took a bite, chewed, and swallowed. They were still the best damn dumplings around. "It's simple. Would you rather sit in the CIA basement working for agents, or would you rather save worlds?"

"This is the kind of thing a man has to think about. One question, though—what will you do if I say no?"

They locked gazes, and Daniel considered lying. The hacker stuffed another dumpling slowly into his mouth, his expression fixed and unwavering.

"I have access to memory wiping drugs. I'll probably stage a bender, call you in as sick, wipe your memory, and you'll wake up the next day wondering what party you went to."

Paul snorted. "That's your plan? It's not a great plan. Shouldn't you have said something like, 'I'll put a bullet in your brain?'"

Daniel's face hardened, and he shook his head. "No, and that's what separates my team from Fortis."

"Okay. We'll see. I'll let you know. Soon." The hacker forked in another mouthful and chewed. "Shame to waste good food in the meantime."

CHAPTER FIVE

There had been no word from Paul yet, but Ronni had said the man ran on his own schedule. He'd answer when he was ready to, one way or the other.

The risk was within Daniel's boundaries. He didn't have a choice, anyway.

The agent adjusted his tie as he walked toward the front door of the shop.

His grandfather stood behind the counter near a set of brass candlesticks with an interesting power. When they held lighted candles, whoever carried one was filled with ideas. Pops was distracted and smiled at something on his tablet. "Trolls playing, love that stuff."

Daniel cleared his throat. "I got a Company message last night. There's a good chance I have to go on a business trip overseas. You have anything you want to clue me in on before I head out?"

You haven't said shit to me. Time to push a little.

Pops looked up with a frown. "What are you talking about?"

The agent waited, his head tilted to the side. "Nothing? We need to have this talk eventually."

The old man grunted and raised his bushy eyebrows but didn't say anything. Daniel headed toward the door.

"Daniel, wait."

He looked over his shoulder. "Yes, Pops?"

"On your way back into town, buy more Fresca and maybe some of those cinnamon Pop-Tarts—enough for the boy *and* me."

Daniel smirked. "Will do."

He strolled into Nessie's office an hour later. She sat behind her cherrywood desk with her hands folded.

"Good morning, Daniel."

"Morning, Nessie. Where am I off to this time?" He closed the door behind him.

"Sweden, specifically Stockholm." She nodded at a briefcase on the corner of her desk. "A few different gadgets this time. An EMP, a jammer, and a refined stun pin." She smiled, pleased with the new devices laid out on her desk. "The jump pad team was happy with your report, and they want you to test them again."

Daniel picked a pen up. Nessie stood and took it gently from him. He raised an eyebrow as she drew a line across her throat. "That's for a different mission. Very deadly. You know better than to touch my things."

"I hope you don't say that to every man you meet."

"I'm not the spinster you like to think I am, and no, it's

none of your business. You'll have to make up my back-story on your own."

"I might not have a chance to try the jump pad again. There aren't a lot of parkour thieves."

Nessie chuckled quietly. "Only if there's an opportunity."

"No chameleon ball this time?"

She pursed her lips. "The device doesn't operate at the desired specifications, so we don't want field agents using it until the kinks are worked out. However, I do have several immobilization capsules for you."

Daniel opened the briefcase and looked inside. "Why, exactly?"

"Field tests suggest they're one of most cost-effective means of restraining magicals, at least until we develop some sort of generic anti-magic technology."

"We could hire magicals, maybe from the PDA. At least they'd be vetted."

Nessie tsked and set the pen carefully on the desk. "I doubt the Senate will agree to that anytime soon. They like the idea of all magicals concentrated in one agency and not in the field—as if they can watch them better that way."

He snorted. "The world has changed. The politicians need to adapt."

"Not that I disagree, but there's little we can do about it *here*." Her glance was sharp, and she turned the case so she could see the contents. "For now, we rely on technology. Between the immobilization capsules and the stun pin, that should be enough."

"You keep dancing around the fact that my target is a magical. What's going on?"

"We've had word of a Wood Elf who calls himself 'the Protector.' He's an ecological extremist." Nessie sighed and shook her head. "While he doesn't actively attempt to harm people, he was involved in several anti-technology incidents that accomplished exactly that. Suddenly disabling all power in the middle of a city results in people getting hurt and killed in car crashes, among other things. Luckily, he hasn't done it near an airport or a hospital, yet. He's demonstrating technology's weakness, hoping humans will turn their back on it."

"Good luck. We like having our refrigerators order takeout." Daniel snorted. "Okay, so my mission is to eliminate this Protector?"

"That's part of it, but we're more concerned about the artifact he recently acquired. It's an ancient kris knife that is allegedly imbued with dark power. In the old days, we'd have called it demonic power."

"A possessed knife."

Nessie laughed, and the wrinkles around her eyes deepened. It wasn't something she often did at work. "That was what the locals thought when their electricity went out. The devil did it. Our information suggests it was a little more vanilla. The knife acts as a rechargeable wide-area EMP. The primary target is the knife. The Protector is secondary."

"Understood." Daniel pointed to several long, opaque, white plastic tubes in the briefcase, careful not to touch anything without an explanation. "What are those?"

She grinned. "Bugs."

"Bugs? Why bother? Why not tap the phones remotely?"

She shook her head, still smiling. "Not that kind of bugs. They're part of an experiment that the SAD is working on with a few other departments. Their nickname is Curious Crawlers—CC for short. They aren't...well, they aren't robots per se. They're a combination of artificially grown insect bioforms and advanced technology." Nessie pursed her lips and waited with her hands open as if to prompt him.

"They're vat-grown cybernetic insects?"

She clapped her hands together. "Bravo! Well done, clever boy. They're excellent at tracking specific smells." She lifted one of the bags and pointed at a tube. "You set the scents using a small spray in one of the tubes. Or, you throw a CC, and it'll sample and transmit to a control source. We'll set that up to be your phone."

"Then what? They swarm like a bad horror movie?"

"I love those movies. Give me a good B-movie with a large insect any day." She chuckled roguishly. "No, they'll trail the smell and transmit their location. Their natural instincts—the bio part we developed—can enhance the operation, and they'll seek out darker locations for natural stealth. If they run out of power or suffer severe damage, they release an anti-enzymatic compound attuned to their exact structure." She waggled her fingers with excitement. "It dissolves their biological components in minutes and interacts with the chemical coating of their other components to destroy them as well."

Daniel laughed at her enthusiasm. "You don't think it'll be suspicious if someone finds a bunch of bugs suddenly melting?"

She shrugged. "It'll merely be a curiosity with no

definitive evidence. These are extremely expensive and still experimental, so don't get too used to them."

"Temptation. Even better." He picked up a tube and opened the lid. Dozens of CCs inside resembled tiny eyeless black beetles. "You think these will help me track down the Protector?"

"It might be your only way."

Daniel replaced the lid gently. "My only way? You don't have confidence in me?"

"Hardly. This particular Wood Elf is renowned for his ability to blend into backgrounds. He's even better at it than most of his kind. He also has something additional that helps him assume different disguises, but we don't have any details on it."

"That is new."

"There's always something. We have intelligence that indicates he'll be at a pub in Stockholm tomorrow to meet a contact. If you can intercept him there and grab the knife, fine, but otherwise, the CCs might help if you can get a scent sample."

"Intel puts the knife on him?"

"Our last report suggests he keeps his favorite artifacts close, and this is one of his most treasured possessions. He despises cities and he won't stay long, so get going. Most of the time, he's in the forest pretending to be a tree—or, for all I know, actually *being* a tree."

Daniel closed the briefcase. "Why do I have a feeling this will be an annoying mission?"

"If that's all it is, you're more badass than even *I* realized."

The agent sipped his Coke as he gazed around the pub. A portly man in a suit smiled at a young woman. They chatted quietly before she patted his hand, stood, and left.

Good, he's alone.

The CIA agent scrolled through a series of images on his phone taken near the Stockholm Arlanda Airport. They depicted a dark-skinned man in a dashiki transforming into a portly, pale man in a suit.

Daniel had been in the right place at the right time. *Coincidence is the universe telling you, "Look here, idiot."*

He didn't plan to engage his quarry in the pub. There were too many people around, and despite what some people thought, confronting dangerous targets in an enclosed area was a bad idea. Having cover was good, but the small room meant he had no space to maneuver.

The portly man dropped a few kronor and stood. He adjusted his jacket, nodded to the approaching waitress, and moved toward the door. Daniel waited for a few seconds, then rose to follow him.

The CIA agent emerged onto the street, stuck his hands in his pockets, and smiled casually to allow the Protector to gain a little distance. With few people on the street, the agent would be noticeable, but to his surprise, his target didn't even look over his shoulder. The portly man did, however, speed up.

Has he made me? Can he see without looking back?

Daniel matched his speed but kept his hands in his pockets.

Maybe that's more suspicious. It's not that cold.

He smirked and withdrew his hands. It wouldn't pay to look *too* obvious.

His target turned a corner, and Daniel had to jog to catch up. The man was already halfway down the block.

Screw it. Now or never.

The agent retrieved one of the CCs and glanced around surreptitiously. No one else was on the street, and the Protector still faced forward. He wound the device quickly, released it, and ducked around the corner. Even if the man noticed what appeared to be a beetle, it only needed a second to generate a scent profile.

He brought the control app up on his Company phone and frowned.

No active units.

Huh? Has he crushed it already? What about the profile?

Daniel tapped a few times.

No stored scent profile.

A smell of something burning filled his nostrils and a second later, his jacket caught fire.

"What the hell?"

He ripped it off and threw it on the ground. Melting CC tubes fell from a charred hole in his pocket, and the devices smoldered. The light green glow around them proved they hadn't malfunctioned.

A spell had traced them back to him. "Sorry, Nessie, I just blew millions of dollars, and we don't even know if it works," he muttered.

Daniel stomped the fire out and shrugged into the damaged jacket. There were still too many other devices in his pockets to leave it there. He hurried to the corner and searched for his target.

I should have used my watch tracker. Then again, I really like this watch and don't need some damn spell to fry it.

Gustav Adolf's Square was about a block away, with its increased traffic, both vehicular and foot. A statue of the king caught Daniel's eye, but there was no sign of the rotund figure. Of course, any one of the dozens of people on the street could be the elf in a new disguise. Without the CCs, he had no way of tracking the Protector.

"Damn it."

A pretty young woman with a backpack looked his way. "Are you all right, sir?" she asked softly, the faintest hint of an accent in her voice. She stared at his burned coat. "Were you in some sort of accident?"

The agent smiled and brushed the ashes off with his sleeve. "Never was a good smoker. I'm fine, thank you. I was…looking for a friend of mine. He lives in this neighborhood, and I thought I saw him. He's on the larger side with dark hair and wore a suit."

She looked over her shoulder and frowned. "I don't think I saw anyone like that. Are you sure you don't need medical attention?"

He shook his head. "No, but I will have some explaining to do to my tailor."

She smiled sympathetically, waved, and walked away. "*Hej då,*" she called.

Daniel moved toward the square and adjusted the jacket to hide the worst of the burns.

He caught a sudden movement from the corner of his eye and spun instinctively, his hand on the stun pin on his tie. John Hollingsworth and two other men in their company jackets stared at him from a short distance away.

"What the hell?"

The tomb raiders sprinted across the light rail tracks. He grabbed an immobilization capsule from his back pocket. While he had no idea what the hell the Hollingsworth men were up to, if they planned to attack a CIA agent, he'd be more than happy to dissuade them.

The men stumbled to a halt a few yards away and frowned. It took Daniel a few seconds to realize they weren't looking at him but to his right and up in the air.

He turned on his heel. The woman who'd seemed so concerned a few minutes earlier now climbed the side of a damned building like Spider-Man.

She's *the Protector? That bastard was taunting me.*

Hollingsworth and his men sprinted toward the building, grapple guns at the ready.

Daniel was right behind them. "I'm beginning to think those should be standard issue on all my missions." The jump pads launched him up the side of the building, and he landed with a painful thud against the hard brick on a tiny ledge.

"Why can't the Swedes make these easier to bounce from?"

A gust of wind almost buffeted him off, but he managed to jump and caught the top of the roof with his fingers. He heaved himself up and rolled to his feet as the tomb raiders crested the roof.

The tomb raider turned his way and blinked. "Bloody hell, Daniel. When did you get here?"

"I could ask you the same thing."

The Protector was already halfway across the roof. The men sprinted after their prey.

Their target leapt to a lower roof. Glowing wings appeared for a moment and smoothed the elf's descent.

"How many devices does he have on him?" yelled Hollingsworth.

His team jumped in pursuit. Two of the men stumbled and clutched the edge to avoid plummeting to the ground. "Keep going," one of them yelled. The rest followed the woman as she raced toward another roof.

Daniel raced side by side with Hollingsworth. "Don't you have to help your guys?" he panted.

The tomb raider laughed and focused on the fleeing Protector. "They can survive a little fall like that. If they couldn't, they wouldn't be retrieval specialists."

The woman jumped across the street, aided once more by her magical wings. Hollingsworth fired his grapple gun, snagged the edge of the roof, and swung. Daniel leapt with the aid of the jump pads and landed a few seconds later. He rolled awkwardly, but at least nothing was broken.

His competitor was already several yards ahead of him.

"Tactical mic? Calling in reinforcements? You okay?" John wouldn't stop to help if he was injured, but he'd call it in. It was professional courtesy in the field.

The Protector suddenly stopped and spun their way. Small squares blurred and flipped over her body. They changed color and texture until an olive-skinned male elf in a loose green tunic replaced the woman. The backpack remained unchanged.

Daniel immediately threw an immobilization capsule at the elf. With astonishing agility, the Protector dodged at the last second. The capsule missed its target and fell onto the street below. The agent yanked the stun pin off his tie.

Hollingsworth stopped and holstered his grapple gun, but he didn't seem eager to close in.

The Protector glanced between the two men. "Your greed has consumed your world, just as it will consume you."

Daniel took a few cautious steps forward. "I don't want the artifact for myself. I'm here to stop you from hurting a lot of people. Spare me the speech."

Hollingsworth snorted but didn't say anything.

"You don't want the artifact?" the elf asked, a mischievous grin on his face. "You don't want to use it for your own corrupt ends?"

The agent sighed and shook his head. "This doesn't have to turn ugly."

The Protector pulled the backpack off. "You want this? Then go get it." He tossed it over the edge of the building and rushed away.

Daniel hesitated for a second, unsure if his adversary was trying to trick him. Hollingsworth jumped off the edge without a moment's thought, his fall broken by a quick shot from his grapple gun.

The CIA agent rushed to the edge of the building and looked down. His competitor opened the backpack. The knife lay inside.

A Hollingsworth Retrieval Specialist SUV screeched to a halt in front of him and the back door flew open.

The tomb raider grinned and waved the backpack. "Sorry, but this is worth a lot to a client. Don't worry, I make sure they're not truly terrible blokes. This is for a private collector." He tossed the backpack into the SUV. "Next round of drinks is on me when I see you at Lucky's."

With a quick, mocking salute, he scrambled into the vehicle and it sped off down the street.

Daniel groaned and looked over his shoulder. The Protector had gone, too.

"Okay, I'm zero for two, and I let a Wood Elf destroy millions of dollars of experimental tech without a real test. Yeah, great day. I could use a Joe Blow."

He shrugged and headed away from the street edge. The building had an inner courtyard that would be less conspicuous when he jumped down.

Lucky's, huh? It's been a while since I've been there.

It was a secure establishment. The owner knew how to enforce the rules, and they also made a mean Manhattan. They liked lowlife high rollers who could follow basic rules. Breaking any of them, even once, meant banishment or worse. No one fucked with Lucky.

The agent leapt off the building. "At least I won't have to pay for the drink."

CHAPTER SIX

Daniel unlocked the back door of the shop and stepped inside, a bag of groceries in hand. He headed for the stairs to the apartment. The door was already open.

"Hey, Pops. I'm back, and I brought a twelve-pack of Fresca and the family-size box of Pop-Tarts."

"Fresca is such an old-man drink," a young voice replied. "And he's not here. He's at some diner in Georgetown. But I'll take a Pop-Tart."

Daniel blinked and turned. His young half-elf friend sat on the living room couch with a biology textbook open in front of him.

"Tommy?"

The teenager grinned. "Mr. Rooney said that since you were in Europe buying stuff, I could stay in your room instead of sleeping on the cot downstairs."

"Did you change the sheets?"

"Of course. I was told it was part of the bargain. Your bed's ready for you."

Daniel made his way to the kitchen and set the groceries down on the old wooden counter. He reached into the bag for an oversized box of Captain Crunch and went to a cabinet near the stove.

"Why do you buy that stuff? That's for you, right? I mean, I get the old man. He has quirks, but you don't strike me as a kid's cereal kind of guy. More of a Grape Nuts man."

"No one is a Grape Nuts man." The agent looked at one of the picture frames that lay face down. "It was my dad's favorite."

"That's cool. I get it." Tommy pulled a guitar pick from his pocket. "Kind of the same thing."

"You're actually doing your homework."

The kid shrugged. "If I want to study robotics and engineering, I need to graduate from high school. That means doing homework."

Daniel laughed. "You can always throw it all away and follow in your father's footsteps."

Tommy shook his head. "No thanks, dude."

The agent finished stowing the groceries and slid the Fresca into the refrigerator before heading down the narrow hallway to his bedroom.

"Hey, Daniel, one question," Tommy called.

He stopped at his door. "Yeah?"

"Why aren't you wearing your jacket? It seems kind of weird to have the rest of the suit on but no jacket." Tommy shrugged.

"I had a little accident and the jacket got burned. Everything's fine now."

The teenager came into the hallway and looked him up and down, confusion on his face.

"Weird buying trip, what can I say?" Daniel headed into his room to slip into some sweatpants and an old Marine Corps T-shirt from boot camp. He stepped out and frowned at the loud knock on the front door.

He found Tommy sitting in the kitchen, an empty plate with a few crumbs in front of him. "Expecting anyone?"

The boy shook his head.

"I'll be right back."

He hurried down the stairs and looked at the front door, half-expecting angry thugs. Instead, he saw a male gnome in an immaculate suit and a matching white fedora.

"Okay, I did not expect that." Daniel blinked and unlocked the door.

"We're closed right now. Come back tomorrow."

"Amusing." The gnome removed his hat, bowed his head, and slipped the hat back on. "Good evening, Mr. Winters."

His exaggerated Connecticut accent was reminiscent of some movie from a hundred and fifty years ago. Even the style of the suit seemed old-fashioned and off.

Maybe this guy has watched too many ancient movies?

Daniel cleared his throat. "Like I said, we're closed for the night."

The gnome nodded solemnly as if every move was part of a ritual. "I would not wish to impose, Mr. Winters, but I've traveled a long way. Would you indulge me with a moment of your time? A friend of mine—a certain over-weight pixie—suggested you might be of assistance—especially considering the history of this shop."

"Madge?" *The history of this shop?* The agent frowned in thought. Was this alien business? He doubted a random gnome had great insight into Fortis or the aliens, but Madge had sent him. She didn't play games.

"Okay, come on in. I didn't catch your name."

The visitor stepped inside. "You can call me Mr. Grant." He inhaled deeply. "Ah, such a great scent. A wonderful place, with so many artifacts. It reminds me of shops on Oriceran."

Daniel closed the door and locked it in case more unexpected visitors showed up. "What do you need, Mr. Grant?"

The gnome didn't respond for several seconds. "A particular item. You might have it. Madge informed me that you have a variety of artifacts available for sale. I didn't realize the store still operated or I would have come some time ago."

Still operated? What does he mean by that?

Mr. Grant strolled to a nearby shelf and picked up a normal-looking pencil. "Do you know what this is?

"An infinite pencil."

The gnome shook his head. "To be clear, this isn't an infinite pencil, but it will last five years. Impressive in its own way." He set the pencil down.

"Huh, I wondered about that."

The visitor moved to the next shelf. He tilted his head and stared at a Theremin. "Do you know what that is?"

Daniel smiled. "That's a genuine antique, one of the original Theremins created by Leon Theremin himself. We know it has some sort of low-level magical power, but we've never been able to figure out what it does other than make spooky music."

His visitor chuckled quietly. He turned a power knob on the instrument and waved his hand between the antennae. Eerie tones emerged from the instrument.

"It doesn't need power? Nice. For some reason, I never thought to test it unplugged."

"It can also potentially control ghosts. You should be careful who you sell it to." He clicked the power knob to Off with a smile.

He turned his head toward the back door, almost as if he could smell the artifacts hidden in the basement vault below. The strange little gnome froze for an agonizing ten seconds before he casually took a red object from a shelf.

Pops had insisted it was nothing more than a flashlight, but Daniel had never been able to get it to work. The only reason they kept it there was that Peter always insisted they weren't a magic shop.

The place was Rooney's Antiquities and Oddities. Sometimes the oddest thing, he claimed, was something normal in a sea of strangeness.

"It's broken," the agent explained. "It's more for ambiance than anything."

Mr. Grant shook his head. He twisted the bottom three times as if to pull it off to change the batteries, then turned it the opposite direction twice. He traced his finger down the shaft. The flashlight clicked on, though the bright lights of the shop concealed the beam.

"There you go," he murmured and held it up. "All working."

"What's this, like an infinite flashlight?"

"No. Not exactly." Mr. Grant pointed it at Daniel. "What do you see?"

Daniel looked down. "Nothing. Should I turn the lights off?"

The gnome shook his head. "Unnecessary." He turned it on himself. A light blue aura surrounded him. "It detects magical beings." He aimed it at the Theremin. Other than destroying the shadow cast by the shelf above, it didn't generate an aura. "But not magic in general. Very valuable to humans. It was created by a half-elf over fifty years ago to aid in tracking down some dangerous magical beings."

Daniel chuckled and shook his head. The entire shop might be filled with magical items that would make the CIA drool. If Fortis had in fact broken into the shop weeks before, they should have stolen everything not nailed down.

"I wish to acquire this item," Mr. Grant declared. "I understand that it has value, so I'm willing to provide something of equal value. This barter is something Mr. Rooney has agreed to in the past."

The agent blinked. "Wait, what? As in, Peter Rooney?"

"Yes. I've never been to this shop before, but I had dealings with him years ago." The gnome pulled his hat off and a worn joker now sat underneath. He offered the playing card to Daniel. "Useful, perhaps."

"What does it do?"

"It persuades a lock to open."

The agent furrowed his brow. "*Persuades* a lock to open?"

"They can be quite reasonable if you know what to say. Simply place the card face down against the lock." Mr. Grant smiled. "It only works five times, but there are few locks on this entire planet it won't open. It is, I think, a fair exchange. You strike me as a man who might occasionally need to open a difficult lock."

Does he know? Given what I've heard, he could be thousands of years old. I've got Daisy on the team. I don't know how worried I am about identifying magicals.

"Deal," Daniel replied. He grabbed the worn card, wondering if it'd prove itself useful sooner rather than later. "Though I want one more thing."

His visitor gave him a toothy grin. "Ah, humans…never satisfied. Always hungry. What is it, Mr. Winters?"

"A funny story about my grandfather." He smiled. "He likes to keep the embarrassing stuff to himself."

If I act casual, maybe he won't realize Pops has kept some things from me.

The gnome snickered. "Ah, indeed. I know a wonderful one. He'd agreed to aid me in a barter situation similar to this one. Our epic quest didn't take us around the world or to Oriceran, but to the five-dollar-and-under aisle at a WalMart in Biloxi, Mississippi. We were led there by a tracking artifact he'd acquired." He clucked his tongue. "For some reason, the artifact I wanted had taken the shape of a pregnancy book. I didn't have any human money on me, so Peter had to pay."

He grinned. "You must understand that back then, this was all new, and humans were deplorably ignorant about most things Oriceran related. The cashier, a lovely woman, congratulated us both on our 'very special blessing.' As the conversation continued, it became apparent that she assumed I was a female gnome, despite my male appearance and a man's suit and hat. Oh, you should have seen your grandfather. He turned a shade of red I didn't know was possible."

He barked a laugh and Daniel joined him. He was only sad his grandfather wasn't there to share the memory.

I'll have to keep that story in my back pocket for the right time. I'll see Pops spew some Fresca then.

Mr. Grant turned the flashlight off with a smile. "Since I have achieved my goal, I must take my leave, Mr. Winters." He removed his hat, bowed his head once more, and replaced it. "May the joker serve you well."

Daniel waited for the gnome to exit and locked the door behind him. It was no secret that his grandfather had done strange things and dealt with odd people to gather some of his antiquities and oddities, but he'd never mentioned Mr. Grant.

Between this, the Munich mission, and that woman, there's a lot more to the OG than I ever realized.

CHAPTER SEVEN

As Daniel made his way toward Timothy's office, he couldn't help but chuckle.

They weren't meeting at the brownstone, so this was official Company business rather than Codex. It reminded him that his day job involved collecting dangerous artifacts or stopping out-of-control magicals, a thought that stirred some amusement.

I sometimes forget how incredible this job is. It's also damned amazing that I'm still alive after all the close calls I've had.

He chuckled all the way to Timothy's office. His mentor waved him inside. For once, he didn't have a stress ball in hand.

"Take a seat, son."

Daniel closed the door behind him and slipped into a chair. The older man didn't have a silence cube or one of Ronni's toys out, and the lack of tension on his face pointed to something unimportant.

"You familiar with Morgana?" Timothy asked.

Daniel frowned. "As in the Morgana from Homeland Security's Enhanced Threats List?"

"Yes, her." Timothy leaned back in his chair. "Did you do something to piss her off?"

"I know nothing about her other than what I've read in government reports. She shows up at remote villages and harvests organs, among other things." Daniel shrugged. "Bad news. Nobody even knows what she looks like."

"She seems to have it out for you."

So much for this not being important.

Daniel blinked. "Huh? How could she have it out for me? I've never even met her."

Timothy shrugged. "So, here's the deal. Her activity was traced to a remote village on one of the southern Philippine islands. The entire village was wiped out. There's no damage to the buildings, but every man, woman, and child is dead, and they were all laid out like they simply went to sleep."

"Organ harvesting?"

The older man shook his head. "No, not this time. No one has any idea what she was doing there, other than killing people."

Daniel frowned. "And what does this have to do with me?"

"Normally, she disappears into thin air and leaves her calling card, a queen of hearts made out of a metal no one has identified yet."

"That's all standard crap. I still don't understand what this has to do with me. Do we have a lead on where she is or what she intends?"

Timothy shook his head. "Nope. Well, sort of."

"Sort of?"

"She used the blood of one of the victims to write on the card." The older man turned his monitor so Daniel could see it. "Here, look for yourself."

The blood-smeared text on the metal playing card clearly read, **Daniel Winters, I'm coming for you.**

"What the hell?" He shook his head. "This doesn't make any sense. I've never worked a case or gone on a mission related to her."

Timothy turned the monitor again. "Are you sure? Maybe you asked about her at some point? You don't have any idea why she might target you?"

"Nope. I've only read about her." He frowned. "So where do we go from here?"

"We'll continue to monitor the situation, but without leads or any more evidence, there's not much we can do. Just watch your back."

Daniel stood. "On the Metro before the last mission, I felt I was being watched. I thought it might be…well, someone else, but maybe it was her."

Timothy frowned. "And since then?"

"Nothing. Maybe she's moved on."

"I wouldn't count on it. We'd never be that lucky."

Daniel snorted and headed for the door. Morgana was a concern, but until she attacked him directly there was little he could do. For now, he'd focus on the trouble right in front of him, including an angry woman in the basement.

As he stepped off the elevator on level B10, Daniel took a

deep breath. He hadn't filed his formal report yet, so Nessie didn't know how badly the field test of the CCs had gone.

At least they now know to be careful around higher-level magicals.

Troy Williams stepped out from a nearby empty cubicle, an obviously fake smile on his face.

"Hey, Winters."

Daniel nodded to him. "Can I help you?"

"You just got back from a mission, right? Stockholm?"

"Yes. What about it?" He maintained his smile and wondered if it looked as fake as it felt. "I need to drop off the borrowed toys and give Nessie a little report."

"Have you done anything else interesting lately?"

Daniel snorted. "You mean other than chase after a Wood Elf who can change his appearance and has a magical EMP knife? Oh, and end up in a chase with a bunch of tomb raiders across the rooftops of Swedish buildings like some well-dressed Mario?"

"You're a real comedian, Winters. Anyone ever tell you that?"

"Lots of people."

Troy leaned in, his smile now feral and vicious. "Shame what happened to Jack Buckley. Especially a shame that we all missed the signs. You and he were buddies, weren't you?"

Daniel shrugged. "I wouldn't say 'buddies.' We never hung out together outside of work. We mostly talked a little shit here and there."

What the hell is this? A test? An interrogation?

Troy scratched his eyebrow. "You know what that whole thing with Buckley taught me?"

"What?"

"That you never really know certain people." The man chuckled and shrugged.

Daniel glanced down at his watch. "Shit. I just realized that there's someone I must talk to before I meet with Nessie. I'll see you around, Williams."

"Yeah, see you around, Winters." Barely-concealed contempt threaded the man's voice.

Daniel turned the corner and headed toward the stairs. He glanced quickly over his shoulder. Troy leaned against a cubicle wall, a smirk on his face like he had all the time in the world to hang around and screw with field agents.

Something in Williams' posture triggered Daniel's inner alarm. The echo of his footsteps filled the stairwell. He took them two at a time, a little test of his mobility. It'd get him closer to his floor and also give him a chance to see if anyone followed him.

It wasn't long before a door thumped closed and other footsteps echoed below him.

The agent stopped, and a few seconds later the footsteps stopped. He started up again.

Old-school. Someone's actually following me? Let's do a little tour of the building and see if they can keep up.

He headed up a few more floors and slipped on some gloves. Calmly, he tapped in the access code, opened the door, and stepped into the hallway.

Daniel reached into a jacket pocket and pressed a button on the back of what looked like a Pokémon card. Next, he retrieved a secondary badge from his wallet, which was linked to a fake ID. It would get him through normal doors without too much trouble, but he couldn't use it for long before the system recognized the deception.

Ronni said her card should obscure my face from the cameras. This is a big damn risk. If I'm caught, it's over. This will stir up a hornet's nest as it is.

The operative continued down the hallway. Muffled gunshots erupted on either side. Bulletproof glass separated the corridor from the multiple agents firing various weapons downrange.

Huh, I almost forgot that my annual firearms qualification is coming up.

He snickered. Shooting and hitting targets wasn't a problem. A suited dark-haired woman opened the glass door in the middle and stepped through, her ear protectors around her neck.

The agent smiled at him and waved. "Hey, Daniel."

He glanced quickly over his shoulder. No one had come in through the stairwell door.

"Hey, Becca. It's been a while."

She shrugged. "Well, we can't all be the special elite messing with magicals. Some of us must content ourselves with simply spying on regular ol' humans."

Daniel chuckled. "Regular ol' humans still have bombs and nukes. That's scary enough."

"You here to practice for your annual qualification?"

He shook his head. "I'm stalling before I go get my ass chewed by Nessie." He held up his briefcase.

Becca laughed. "Yeah, that's what playing around with SAD agents will get you." She patted him on the shoulder.

"I need to squeeze off a few more rounds. Talk to you later."

Daniel nodded, and the agent stepped into the firing range and slipped her ear protection on. With no obvious pursuit in sight, he hurried to the stairs at the opposite end of the hallway and headed up.

He threw the door open and stepped onto the new floor. An agent he didn't recognize frowned at him.

Did they switch off? Would they really use tradecraft on me inside the building?

Daniel frowned. Had Becca intercepted him to create a delay so the next tail could get into position?

He took a deep breath and released it slowly. It was easy to think that those who worked for Fortis radiated hostility like Troy Williams, but he couldn't trust anyone. The CIA was filled with spies, men and women who'd been trained to conceal themselves and become different people.

Paranoia was part of the business. Sometimes it saved you, and sometimes it cost you.

Daniel took a moment to look around. He hadn't paid much attention when he stepped onto the floor, and he usually took the elevator to the firing range. A series of large metal chambers dominated the area with a wide passage between. The rooms were separated from the corridor by thick walls and metal doors, and a bright display identified their contents. The first was labeled, Outer Beijing Energy Weapons Testing Ground.

A sense of nostalgia attacked him—the VR training rooms. He hadn't been in one in years. There was no point in checking inside. All anyone would see was a bunch of people in helmets and bodysuits moving around a featureless white room. He'd trained for more than a few missions in these rooms when he'd first been recruited.

He continued past other simulation rooms, including the Pyongyang Artifact Experimentation Lab, the Moscow Advanced Propulsion Laboratory, the New York Oriceran Embassy, and one that genuinely surprised him, Unnamed Concealed Iowa Gnome Enclave.

There's a gnome enclave in Iowa? Is that why they have so many tornadoes?

The stairwell door behind him squeaked open. Daniel didn't bother to look, instead heading toward the elevator. He stepped inside and hit the Close button with a smile. He spotted the shadow agent through the gap as the doors sealed.

"Too bad, pal." He selected a sub-basement level and entered a code. With a grimace, he retrieved what looked like the tip of a thumb from his inner pocket.

This is as good a time as any to test this. Ronni swore it isn't actually a thumb, but it sure feels like one.

Daniel pressed the macabre artifact against the DNA scanner and waited. From what Ronni had explained, she'd used the fact that they still hadn't cleared Jack Buckley's DNA profile from the system.

Neither Ronni and Daniel doubted that security would figure it out sooner or later, but for now, a ghost with a fake ID wandered CIA headquarters. Even if Troy and the agents tailing him were with Fortis, they couldn't prove anything.

He chuckled as the elevator descended. When it opened, he stepped off and rushed through a series of passages. He didn't know this level well, and the featureless doors marked only with numbers didn't provide any insight into where he might be.

His adventure came to an end at a huge reinforced door with a keypad and a DNA scanner. He tried his fake credentials, and neither worked.

Should I try the joker? I only have five uses.

Daniel wasn't sure why he felt compelled to place the card against the mysterious door. His only explanation was that years of instinct combined with paranoia made him want to know what was on the other side. The keypad beeped, and the massive bolts thudded as they retracted.

He tugged on the door and stepped inside. A series of reinforced windowless doors lined a narrow hallway. The floor was mostly metal grating. Displayed to the side of the first door, near the keypad and DNA scanner, was a head-shot of a scowling man.

He looks familiar.

Daniel leaned in to read the name beneath the picture: Anton Vinzetti. He recognized the name. The man'd had a short-lived but lucrative career trafficking nuclear weapons.

The cell across from him was home to a Light Elf named Saram. The agent didn't know the face, but he'd read a report about a high-grade elf assassin who some-times went by that name.

He continued his exploration. While he didn't know all the names or pictures, he recognized many as dangerous terrorists and enemy agents, both human and Oriceran.

An entire fucking high-security prison directly beneath head-quarters? Who the hell knows about this? And haven't these idiots ever opened a comic book? They didn't put Belle Reve in the Watchtower. They're asking for trouble.

Another massive door at the far end was marked Hangar Twelve. He tried his fake ID, but again, it didn't work. A large reinforced one-way viewing port allowed him to see inside.

The large room contained more prisoners—human, he immediately thought, but their skins were covered with strange symbols that shifted like living ink. He couldn't be sure from this distance, but some might resemble the alien symbols he'd previously encountered.

So, they not only have a secret ultramax down here but also an alien holding pen?

Daniel shook his head and stared at the prisoners. They were emaciated and looked exhausted, and, for the most part, more frightened than fierce.

Shit. I need to get out of here before someone decides to check why the main door opened.

He turned and sprinted back through the prison. Thankfully, the massive door was still open. He stepped through and closed it, and the bolts automatically shot into position to seal the prisoners inside with a menacing whump.

Daniel navigated back to the elevator. Once inside, he pressed a button for a level two floors up from where his desk was located. He had no reason to make things easy for those tailing him or to see Nessie right away.

I'll have to ask Ronni to make a new fake badge for me. If this one isn't crap within an hour, the CIA doesn't know what they're doing.

He took several deep breaths and tried to calm his

pounding heart. For some reason he'd convinced himself Fortis would hide their activities far from Company headquarters, but then again, they probably never expected some curious man to show up with a universal key.

One question haunted him.

Why are they shadowing me so closely? If they think I'm compromised, why not simply take me out? Or is this just intended to make me nervous?

CHAPTER EIGHT

John Hollingsworth was in town for a night, and he wanted to get together for a drink later that evening at Lucky's. Having a round or two with the tomb raider made Daniel want to laugh.

I guess a man like me can have a night out with friends, even if they are possible intelligence agents for other countries and steal artifacts out from under me.

First, though, he had a few items of business to handle.

The agent slipped his phone into his pocket as he headed to Timothy's brownstone office. He'd spent most of the day doing paperwork at the CIA. Troy Williams hadn't bothered him again, nor did anyone else.

As much as he wanted to take comfort in that, it didn't prove they weren't spying on him. If anything, he was convinced that the only reason they'd used physical tails in the building was to unnerve him. Intelligence and psychological warfare were CIA specialties, after all.

Timothy sat behind his desk and squeezed his stress ball. He spoke as Daniel took a seat. "I looked into things after you sent me your message. As far as I can tell, no one's planning an immediate move against you, at least not using aboveboard CIA procedures like they did with Ronni. If anything, I don't think they would have played their little game if they wanted to eliminate you right now. It might not even be what you think."

"Maybe." Daniel shrugged. "But they definitely didn't want to give me a free ice cream cone."

His mentor slipped the stress ball into his desk and ran a hand across his bald head. "Or it was a test. Maybe they want you for Fortis, and they wanted to see how you'd react under stress when threatened at headquarters."

The younger agent laughed. "Yes, just what I need—another layer of false identities."

"It's a possibility, son. We'll figure out how to handle it if and when it happens."

Daniel nodded. "What do you think about the rest of my message?"

Timothy shrugged. "I'm surprised that they'd risk so much with a de facto ultramax below headquarters, let alone incarcerate aliens there, but these are people who destroyed a town as a cover-up." He sighed. "I suspected one, if not several, facilities of this kind existed, but not the actual location."

"And you never knew about it?"

He chuckled darkly. "I'm watched closely, son. Even with all my insurance and backup plans, I couldn't pull off what you did."

Daniel leaned forward and kept his voice low. "Will we make a move against that place?"

"Not anytime soon." Timothy raised his hand to placate

him. "Those might be innocent alien tourists, but we don't know for sure. They're hidden behind maximum CIA security. I might not have known about Hangar Twelve, but the black site isn't as secret. Trust me. If it's this hush-hush, everyone else deserves to be there."

"Maybe, but those people or aliens in Hangar Twelve didn't look deadly." Daniel shrugged. "They look defeated, starved, and exhausted."

The older agent sighed and nodded. "Okay, I'll try to find out more without risking a bullet, but until I know more, we do nothing. They might be tired right now, but maybe all they need is to drink a little blood or something to rejuvenate. We can't start a rampage across D.C. that kills every human. And let's be realistic—even if they weren't angry before, incarceration might have now made them hostile. We need to know both their intentions and their abilities."

Daniel frowned. "I thought you said that the point of our little group, among other things, was to stop a war of the worlds. Locking up innocent aliens doesn't seem proactive."

Timothy sighed and rested his head on the back of the chair. "I need more information before we do anything that impacts the security of this country and this planet. If they aren't dangerous, we'll find a way to spring them that won't get the innocent killed, whether alien or human. Agreed?"

Daniel nodded. "Fair enough."

Timothy exhaled slowly and leaned forward. "Besides, I have a more immediate concern. I'll brief the others soon, but you're taking point so you need the details first." He frowned as he gathered his thoughts. "A lucky break has given us an opportunity to get ahead of the game instead of simply reacting."

"What are you talking about?"

His mentor's dry chuckle sounded weary. "We have information about a mass alien sighting. I can suppress it for a few days, but eventually, it'll leak to the CIA and Fortis. My concern is this isn't a few people but the entire tiny rural town of Aaronstown in central Michigan. The people say they saw strange lights in the skies and unusual aircraft. Some claim to have seen aliens."

Daniel shrugged. "So? It could simply be drones on parade or Oricerans playing tricks. Come on. I saw tons of similar reports even before I joined your team. The only time it was remotely interesting was when the Willen had some sort of contest while high on dust."

Timothy shook his head. "Reports I've intercepted from the NRO and other agencies mention detecting strange activity. It might be Oricerans, but the initial PDA reports indicate minimal magic in the area so they won't bother to investigate. Evidence indicates non-Oriceran extraterrestrials. The point is that our group has a head start."

The younger man frowned thoughtfully. "Do we know where the aliens are? You mentioned aircraft. Did anyone see them land?"

"The reports conflict and nothing is confirmed. This is your next mission, and I want you there by tomorrow. We'll play this low-key. Evaluate the situation and identify possible actionable intelligence. This could be a contact situation, an artifact retrieval, or even a mission of mercy. Get the information from those townspeople."

Daniel scratched his cheek. "If I go there, won't they tell people later about men in black showing up? Won't that get them on TV and make things worse?"

Timothy shrugged. "Wear a blue suit, then. Have you ever heard someone bitch about a man in blue?"

It probably hadn't been one of Daniel's smarter ideas to return to the CIA in the middle of the night, but so far, no one had bothered him. If Fortis or whoever had stalked him believed he was trouble, they wouldn't kill him in or near headquarters. If they tried, he would make it a costly mistake.

I'm not Ronni. I'm a field agent and a Marine veteran. They know that and have to plan accordingly.

The point of his return visit was to lay a little bait and misdirect the enemy. Ronni had seeded several false reports of unusual magical artifacts in Chile. Daniel wanted to convince anyone reviewing his computer's activity logs that he had gone there. Fortis might even send an agent on a wild goose chase and squander valuable time.

The operative grinned at that happy possibility as he sent an email to Nessie about possible equipment for his Chilean jaunt. After a satisfying stretch, he surveyed the mostly empty cube farm, alert for Troy Williams or other unusually suspicious people.

He locked his computer and headed for the elevator. The door closed, and he allowed himself a smile. The situation was exciting despite the tension that came with outwitting Fortis, both inside or outside the CIA. An exemplary secret government agent enjoyed the challenge of putting his skills and his life on the line.

I'm not an adrenaline junky, but I like winning against worthy opponents. These guys are assholes, but they aren't pushovers.

The elevator stopped a few floors up, and another man stepped in. He had a downcast expression on his face. The doors closed with a ding, and it took Daniel's brain a few seconds to register the impossible. Only a living Jack Buckley or his parents would have surprised him more. The CIA agent's eyes widened, and his heart rate kicked up.

"Connor?"

The blond dungeon master blinked a few times and stared at him. "What the hell?"

Daniel snapped his arm up and pressed a button for a floor lower than the lobby. "Don't say anything here, but we need to talk."

The two men avoided eye contact until the elevator arrived at the new destination.

"Follow me," Daniel ordered and stepped out.

Connor complied, more confused than upset. Daniel found an empty conference room, opened the door, and motioned his friend inside.

Once they were seated, he activated his silence cube and set it on the table. With none of Ronni's toys to help, he'd need to watch what he said in case anyone tried to lip-read the video later.

I don't want to get either of us into trouble.

Daniel stared at his friend. "What the hell are you doing here?"

Connor snorted. "I'm an intelligence analyst with top secret clearance and an assload of caveats."

"Yeah, but you're a SIGINT guy, not a HUMINT guy. You're supposed to work with NSA, not CIA."

The other man shrugged. "Some things are multi-jurisdictional." He frowned. "But you already know that." He pointed at the ID badge on Daniel's jacket and squinted to read it. "You're a high-level agent."

Daniel ran his hands through his hair and took a deep breath. Given his security clearance, he paid no attention to direct sourcing anymore. He wasn't an analyst, so he only wanted actionable intelligence. By the time it reached him, every alphabet intelligence agency on the planet and all their analysts had probably had input.

"I can explain…" he began, then paused.

Connor's frown vanished and was replaced by a huge grin. "You sonofabitch. You had us all fooled. Oh, Daniel merely runs his shop and occasionally protects old ladies from muggers. Shit, I always thought that whole 'mayor' thing was because you were bored." He laughed. "You should get a damned Oscar for your performance. We all sat around thinking, 'Oh, poor Daniel, can't be satisfied running his granddad's shop.' Meanwhile, you're CIA and are probably arranging some coup on Oriceran."

Daniel groaned. "How do you know I'm not a HUMINT analyst?"

His friend smirked and pointed to the silence cube. "I'm not a field agent, but I recognize the toys. No way in hell would they give some desk jockey an omnidirectional sonic nullifier."

The CIA agent scowled. "Ugh. I hate that name. Call it a silence cube."

"A silence cube?" Connor laughed. "Geeze, that's so fucking lame. Is every field agent as bad as you?"

"It's quicker to say, at least." Daniel smiled sheepishly. "But, yeah, I'm a field agent, and I work mostly on dangerous artifact collection. You *do* realize you can't tell anyone?"

Connor rolled his eyes. "Yeah, it's not like I work in intelligence, have a security clearance, or know anything about that. Don't worry, I'll keep my mouth shut. You know, you didn't have to hide it. You could have pretended to be an analyst at the CIA. It's not like we would pester you for details."

The agent shook his head. "It's easier and safer for everyone this way. We also shouldn't openly acknowledge each other if we meet here in the future."

The other man sighed. "Don't worry. I doubt I'll ever be back at CIA headquarters after the humiliation I just suffered. Fuckers."

"Humiliation?"

Connor glanced at the cube. "You got that out, so I should be honest. I was dumb, anyway, when I hinted about it during our game. I worked a project—unusual signals analysis off some satellite intercepts. Originally we thought the Chinese or Russians were messing around, but the signals used bands that no one typically chooses for communication. And then, well…" He groaned. "This will sound stupid and unbelievable."

Daniel shrugged. "Try me. I collect magic artifacts for a living. That would have sounded stupid twenty years ago."

"I'll spare you the boring technical details. Anyway, I convinced myself that it was, you know…aliens."

The agent looked surprised. "Aliens? Oricerans?"

"No, no. You know, *alien* aliens. The kind from outer space—big tech, FTL, all that crap." Connor scrubbed a hand over his face. "I convinced my supervisor, and everybody in my department thought, 'Wow, we've just proved the existence of aliens. That's a big deal, even with Oriceran.' Since I was the main analyst, I had to give a big fancy presentation at the CIA to several agencies' representatives. We thought NSA would be at the heart of some badass alien task force with some cool name, like Project Sagan or Project Celestial."

Shit. Will Fortis come after Connor now?

"And?" Daniel asked, keeping his voice neutral. "What happened at your presentation?"

Connor shrugged. "And nothing. I spent hours on the analysis and tried to exclude possibilities and a bunch of crap like that—standard intelligence protocol. I gave the briefing, and they basically shredded me like a virgin analyst fresh out of tech training. It turns out it's some stupid Light Elf collection shit. The CIA keeps it hush-hush due to a freaking bilateral agreement with the fucking elves. One asshole even went so far as to call me Mulder Jr. and laughed in my face." He shook his head. "Some douchebag named Williams."

"Troy Williams?"

"Yeah, you know him?"

Daniel nodded, his stomach tightening. "Yeah. He *is* a douchebag. Sorry."

Connor chuckled. "It doesn't matter. What does matter

is that since your buddies at the CIA didn't provide this information earlier, I wasted a shit ton of time. Worse, it'll be a while before I'm assigned any future special projects."

"But you're okay otherwise? No one's threatened you, right?"

The man blinked with surprise. "Threatened me? No. They simply made it clear that before I push for a big meeting, I should cross-check all official channels." He sighed with evident frustration. "My boss is sympathetic, though. She says this shit happens and no one in my department will hold it against me. Apparently, she had something similar happen with some DoD satellites early in her career. It might be safer all around, but compartmentalization leads to crap like this."

Daniel frowned. "It's not your fault, Connor. It's the CIA's for not reaching out to your team. They're the ones who wasted everyone's time."

"You're damned right." He stood and nodded. "Look, thanks, Daniel, but I must go. I need to get back to my office to clean this mess up, and you have to assassinate some gnome princess or something."

"I'm sorry about all this, Connor."

His friend headed toward the door with a wave.

Daniel remained in his chair and scowled as the other man left. He didn't believe for one moment that his friend hadn't found the truth.

Don't think I'll thank you Fortis assholes because you didn't kill my friend. I get it—you couldn't. He'd told too many people. With a dead analyst, all those people dripping security clearances would suspect foul play and a cover-up, so you tried to assassinate his career instead.

His boss and coworkers might not give him trouble, but you assholes tried. Everything you do makes this personal.

Daniel stood, retrieved his silence cube, and stomped to the door with a snort. He had an early day tomorrow, but that didn't mean he couldn't use a little drink.

CHAPTER NINE

The agent smiled at the partially burned-out L CKY S
B R neon sign above the door.

He stepped inside. Rough-looking people and the occasional adventurous businessman were drinking at various
tables. Daniel ignored them and the pretty bartender and
headed to the men's room.

The restroom was surprisingly clean. He moved toward
the stall closest to the far wall. Someone inside whistled
cheerfully.

Why did they have to choose this one?

Daniel folded his arms and leaned against the wall.

About two minutes later, the occupant flushed and
opened the door. He frowned and looked at the other open
stalls.

"You could have used one of those, pal."

The agent shrugged. "That's my lucky stall. I don't like
using the others."

The man's face contorted in disgust. "What does luck
have to do with it?"

"What can I say? I'm really into my rituals."

"Freak." He rolled his eyes and stomped off without washing his hands.

You're the inconsiderate one, asshole.

Once the door closed, Daniel entered the stall and locked it. He rotated his hand against the wall and murmured, "I, Daniel, do solemnly swear I'm not an asshole. Just ask Lucky."

A faint hiss sounded, and the two sides of the wall separated slightly. He pulled the edges farther apart until he could step through and headed down a stairwell lit by dim red lights.

More submarine lighting? I hope that's not the universe trying to tell me something.

On the fourth step, the wall snapped shut behind him and a click echoed in the stairwell. The bathroom stall unlocked automatically at the same time.

Daniel smiled at the juxtaposition of Italian opera music and the dingy walls. Many people complained about access to the real Lucky's through a bathroom stall, but he loved it. It was the kind of thing he'd always imagined as a kid. The ladies' room had a similar one, but they didn't complain as much.

The stairwell opened into the large main bar area. Round tables packed tightly around the room were barely illuminated by the low lighting. Shadows were their own decor at Lucky's.

The chatter of patrons filled the air. Dangerous men with scarred faces drank alongside smiling men in slick suits. A gnome sat near the back in a gray suit. Several elves occupied another table and tossed dice containing invisible magic. Lucky didn't care what species you were, but he did like high rollers—provided he received his cut.

Drinks were served by beautiful waitresses of various species clad in skirts that defied even the most charitable application of the word.

The place occupied a gray zone between a private club and a secret public bar. Lucky welcomed those involved in dangerous and borderline trades, whether tomb raiding, directly criminal, or vaguely aboveboard like the CIA. Other than that, he had a primary rule, Rule #0, for potential membership: Don't be an asshole.

The "suggested annual donation" wasn't technically a rule, but no one wanted to find out what Lucky might do if you tried to enter without paying after your first visit. The Company paid for Daniel's membership since they considered the bar a useful though unorthodox source of intelligence.

Guards stood in the darkened corners of the room, assault rifles strapped to their backs. At least one man wore a holstered wand. In Lucky's Bar, his rule was law, and he didn't like trouble. Daniel had witnessed his men kill a troublemaker without blinking. Allegedly, Lucky had a special contract with Purity Solutions to handle the disposal of bodies.

It wasn't hard to avoid being a troublemaker. Lucky had rules beyond not being an asshole. Although there were a lot of them, Daniel had heard the first three most often.

Rule #1: All grudges or missions are dropped at the door. No battles or deaths are allowed unless Lucky or his men do the killing.

Rule #2: No one leaves without buying at least one drink.

Rule #3: Luciano Pavarotti is the greatest tenor of all time, and anyone who disagrees must leave immediately.

Some poor fool had tried to argue for Placido Domingo the last time Daniel was there and barely escaped with his life. Daniel wasn't sure if Lucky truly believed Pavarotti was better or if his Italian pride wouldn't acknowledge a Spaniard as superior. Oddly enough, he accepted that Craddan, an elf singing with the New York Metropolitan Opera, might be a close second. Daniel, for his part, had no strong opinions on opera.

The agent glanced at several names etched into the wall above the bar. Most people claimed they were the names of Lucky's favorite patrons who had passed away, but rumor said they had all died because they broke a rule. The man could like you and still kill you. Rules were rules.

Lucky stood behind the wooden bar with a broad smile on his face. A pinstripe suit draped his huge frame. He was taller than most men, but Daniel still had some height on him. The owner looked good for a man in his fifties, although he dyed his hair and slicked it back too aggressively.

"Daniel, long time no see, *paisan*. I worried that you thought you were too good for my place." Lucky clucked his tongue.

"If anything, I think I'm not good *enough* for your place."

He barked out a laugh. "You're such a great guy. You sure you're not Italian?" His hands moved animatedly with each word.

"I'm a lot of things, depending on the day."

"You should stick to being Italian. We've got women, cooking, music, history, and the language."

The agent studied the room and smiled when his gaze landed on a leather-clad female elf in the corner. Daisy. She raised her glass and nodded.

Even though she'd agreed to join the team, she wasn't ready to take her marching orders from Timothy or Daniel. She'd made it clear that she would help them when and how she felt like it. Neither CIA agent could break her of habits she'd depended on for longer than either of them had been alive.

"I've got to talk to Daisy, Lucky. Will you send a Manhattan my way when you get a chance?"

"Sure, pal. Like I said, good to see you again. Heard you almost got carved up by the New Veil in Canada, and then I didn't see you. I was a little worried." Lucky shrugged. "You never know. Live by the sword, die by the portal."

Daniel gave him a quick nod and headed toward Daisy. When he'd first visited the bar, Lucky had surprised him by knowing things he shouldn't. After the shock wore off, the CIA agent realized that it made him a useful source of knowledge.

Daisy smiled as he took a seat across from her. "To what do I owe the pleasure?"

"I'm here to get a drink John Hollingsworth owed me."

"For snagging an artifact out from under you?"

Daniel chuckled. "He got lucky."

Daisy grinned. "Too late. He was here earlier, but something came up. He and a few of his guys raced out of here."

"Maybe he's only in the States for a tomb raid." The

agent shrugged. "Might as well ask around about an upcoming job while I'm here."

She sipped her drink delicately. "A job? You're not here for *me*?" The pout was realistic. "I'm almost disappointed." She ran her finger around the rim of her glass. "Maybe I'm losing my charm."

Daniel chuckled. "No, never. You're merely more woman than I can handle—not to mention the age difference, you gorgeous cradle-robber."

She winked. "I've had time to practice certain skills."

"I'll bet."

A waitress arrived with a Manhattan and set the drink on the table. "Your drink, sir."

Daniel smiled at her. "Thank you."

After the girl sauntered off, Daisy leaned back. She licked her lips and smiled. "Tell me about your job."

"Strange sightings in Michigan. Some people claim it's aliens."

"Yes, I heard about that, but it wasn't something I saw profit in, so I haven't dug into it." She ran her tongue over the inside of her cheek. "Is this something you need…help with, or is this a Company matter? Of course, I'll work for them too if they pay my fee."

Daniel took a few breaths. His instinct was to grab his silence cube, but that would violate Rule #4: No disguises, and no silence magic or devices are allowed. That didn't necessarily leave him vulnerable. Lucky didn't care if you overheard something, but Rule #5 made things fair: No bugs or spying magic.

He leaned in to whisper to his companion. At least the

quiet background opera rather than blasting pop music meant they didn't have to shout.

"We're ahead of the Company on this. Normally, I'd say I want your help, but in this case it might be better to keep you in the background in case things go south. It's good to have a few surprises, and you're a very surprising person."

The elf snickered and nodded toward a dark corner across the room. "Ralph might know more. He mouthed off about something in Michigan earlier." She winked. "And if you change your mind about needing help, give me a buzz." She held his gaze as she sipped languidly.

Daniel took a sip or two, then stood and headed toward the corner booth.

Ralph had a half-filled glass in front of him and wore a wide smile, but his face was as red as Mars. The agent resisted a snort. The man had always been a human wreck, and his fancy new suit didn't match his drunken, disheveled appearance. That said, even a fly on garbage might overhear something useful now and then.

The operative sat without asking permission and set his drink on the table. "What're you drinking tonight, Ralph?"

The other man grinned and revealed two gold teeth. "The Nomad."

"The Nomad? I don't think I've heard of that one."

"Vodka, lemonade, grenadine, and Fresca." Ralph laughed.

What? Are you related to Connor and Pops?

"I think I'll stick to Manhattans." The agent raised his drink in a mock toast.

I wonder why Lucky specializes in Manhattans when he's from Brooklyn? I'll remember to ask him sometime.

Ralph patted his stomach. "Really hits the spot when you're celebrating."

Daniel nodded. "I notice you have a new suit. I never did figure out how the hell you can afford the membership in a place like this, but you're usually not dressed so nicely. I always figured you had to spend all your money on the suggested donation."

His companion snorted and gulped down more of his drink. "I've got money and sources you couldn't even begin to understand, but yeah, I've had a recent windfall. It's one of the reasons I'm celebrating."

"And would this little windfall have anything to do with Aaronstown, Michigan?"

Ralph laughed loudly, and spittle settled on his lips. "Maybe. Maybe not. I'm a busy man living a busy life. It's hard to keep track of everything I do."

"Let's cut the bullshit and get to business. I want to know what you know about Aaronstown and what you want for the info."

The man set his glass down and looked cautiously at him. "Whatcha got to give to me?"

The two men stared each other down. Daniel reached into his pocket for what looked like a small stuffed panda and tossed it to his companion.

"What the hell is this?" Ralph eyed the toy.

The agent shrugged. "A listening device, but I can't demonstrate it here without pissing Lucky off. The button is concealed in the back, along with a frequency modulator. It has great range and decent transmission penetration, even in areas where you normally can't transmit."

There's no reason to let him know it's one of Ronni's little mixes of tech and low-level magic.

Ralph chuckled and examined the toy. "This is pretty fucking funny. What are you supposed to spy on with this, some kid's birthday party?"

"There are suspicious kids out there these days." Daniel grinned.

The other man snickered. "Yeah, okay, fair enough. I'm sure I can find a use for it." He sniffed and wiped his nose. "See, I don't know a lot about Michigan, but the locals claim they saw something in the sky. I figured it was some Oriceran bullshit, but that's not the interesting part."

"What is the interesting part?"

Ralph leaned in to whisper. "They left something behind. Some sort of weapon—a rocket or some shit, but it doesn't go boom. It *changes* shit."

"Changes things? How?"

"Rearranges it. Mixes it up. One idiot tried to see how it worked and accidentally shot one of his cows with it. It ended up twisted like some weird-ass painting or something."

The agent had a flashback to the distorted body in Munich. It took all his self-control not to wince.

He shrugged and kept his expression blank. "Interesting. That all?"

Ralph shook his head. "Nope. The local hicks still have it, but they buried it. From what I hear, they can't decide what to do with it."

"Why not ask the government to take it?"

The other man barked a laugh. "Haven't you heard what the nine scariest words in the English language are?"

Daniel snorted. "I'm from the government, and I'm here to help."

Ralph gulped the rest of his Nomad, set his glass on the table, and stood. He pocketed the panda and gave Daniel a mock salute. "I have some shit to take care of. Nice doing business with you."

The agent nodded and leaned forward to rest his arm on the table and his chin in his hand.

Another damned molecular rearrangement weapon. One was bad enough. How many of these do the aliens have?

He knocked the rest of his drink back and shook his head. He needed to get to that weapon before Fortis decided another small town was acceptable collateral damage.

CHAPTER TEN

Daniel walked toward his shop with his hands in his pockets. He'd already purchased a plane ticket, but he wanted to check on things before he headed out of town. For all he knew, he could be gone for a day or for weeks.

Several old men from the neighborhood stood on the sidewalk and stared at the ground. They'd all been retired for almost as long as he'd been alive.

Fred pointed at the paving. "Hurry up, Carter. Your turn."

A few dimes lay near a separation line in the sidewalk, one slightly closer to the other.

Daniel chuckled.

I guess when you're retired, you have to stay busy any way you can. Keep doing that while you can, guys. At the rate we're going, we might not have physical currency in a few years.

Carter knelt with a loud groan. "My knees aren't made for this anymore."

Will snorted. "What are you whining about, old man? I

know you got some fancy new knees a few years back."

"'Old man?' I'm three years younger than you."

Carter squinted and set a dime atop his thumb. He took several deep breaths and flicked the metal. The coin sailed in a graceful arc, turned several times, and landed on the line.

He snatched up the three dimes with a grin. "I'm the champion, guys."

The other two men sketched mocking bows and chanted in unison, "All hail the glorious champion."

Daniel chuckled, shook his head, and moved on. Maybe his D & D group should try a coin-flicking competition in their next For Want of a Dollar challenge.

He approached the shop. A large, TEMPORARILY CLOSED, TRY AGAIN TOMORROW sign hung in the window.

The agent unlocked the door and stepped in without turning the sign.

I wonder if anyone other than Connor will eventually figure out the truth? I'm gone so often that they must at least suspect something. Or maybe they don't. Most people are more than willing to believe what they think they see unless you give them a reason to think otherwise.

With that thought, he marched up the stairs to the apartment to pack a suitcase.

Thirty minutes later, Daniel walked downstairs to find Tommy leaning against the counter while he read a comic.

The boy looked up with a smile. "Hey, Daniel."

"Hey, Tommy."

The half-elf's gaze dropped to the suitcase. "Oh, going on another buying trip? I swear you spend more time out of the shop than in it, dude."

"Yeah, it does seem that way sometimes."

The teen set the comic on the counter and straightened. "Mr. Rooney's supposed to be retired."

"That's an accurate statement." Daniel chuckled. "Why do you mention it?"

Tommy shrugged. "I could watch the store for you this time. That way, he doesn't have to worry about it. He can just, you know, be retired."

Daniel set his suitcase down and hugged the boy around the neck. "One of these days I'll have to give you a full-time job." He pulled away with a grin.

"You mean it?"

"Yeah. One of these days. Not today." The agent shook his finger. "But I'd like any future employees to at least have a high-school education. You don't need to worry about this shop. We've got enough money that I could have it open once a week and be fine."

Tommy rolled his eyes. "Yeah, but you spend it all on buying more weird stuff, dude."

Daniel ruffled his hair. "This isn't negotiable. School first. Always."

"Okay." The boy leaned against the counter again and picked up the comic.

The door opened and Peter stepped through. He glanced from the suitcase to his grandson and grunted.

The old man started toward the back but stopped half-way. "I've got time later to help you with your clock for that school project, Tommy. I owe you for picking up more Fresca for me."

The boy smiled. "Thanks, Mr. Rooney."

Peter waved and disappeared into the back room.

Daniel stared at the door for a moment.

Helping a gnome find an artifact is one thing, but contact with aliens is a whole different matter. Maybe Timothy was right, and that woman merely had psychic power. Could it have been a desperate pull on something from my memory as a last resort?

He blew out a breath and shook his head. "See you in a few days, Tommy."

Daniel took the exit for Aaronstown, Michigan. His high school had more people than the entire town, judging by the listed population.

"I hate tiny towns," he muttered.

"Why?" Ronni asked in his ear.

His heart rate sped up, and he jumped a little in his seat. He'd forgotten she was on the comm. Their last conversation had been right before he boarded a plane at Reagan National. Worried that she hadn't tested the effects of her communication gear during flights, she'd suggested they go dark until he landed.

"You surprised me." Daniel shook his head. "It's weird to always have a girl in your ear."

Ronni laughed. "Sorry. I've been busy, and didn't pay much attention until the last few minutes. What do you have against small towns?"

"Oh, that?" Daniel chuckled. "Nothing, normally, but they're terrible for missions. It's hard enough to remain unnoticed in a large city, especially if it's not one you're familiar with. But a city has thousands, if not millions, of people. In a little town, everyone knows everyone, and any stranger stands out. That makes people suspicious, so it's hard to get what you need."

"Oh, that makes sense."

Daniel turned onto the main road. "It's good to have backup, though. I don't think I'll have too much trouble, but with Morgana targeting me, I can't be too careful."

Ronni sighed. "You don't think it's because we talked about her, do you? If she's some sort of witch, maybe it's a Bloody Mary thing."

He laughed. "I doubt that. She could have a spell like that, but you'd think she'd focus on Homeland Security or bounty hunters like that guy Brownstone in LA, not random CIA agents."

"You're not afraid of her, are you?"

He snorted. "See, this is where people get confused. Panic is wrong, but fear is healthy. If you're not afraid, you end up dead like Pickett's division at Gettysburg. A little healthy fear means you recognize threats and deal with them. In this job, when I stop being afraid, I'll end up as sushi for some creepy magical."

Ronni gagged. "Did you really have to put it that way?"

"It got the point across, didn't it?"

"Yes, but it'll probably give me nightmares, and I don't think I'll be able to eat sushi for a while."

Daniel chuckled. "Well, let's talk about something else, then."

"Okay," Ronni replied. "Have you heard from Paul?"

He frowned, thankful she couldn't see him. "Not yet. *Should* I have heard from him? More to the point, should I be worried?"

"I've monitored things, and Timothy and Nessie have kept their eyes open at the Company."

"The whole reason we want this guy is because he's one of the best hackers in the world," Daniel replied. "I'm not sure we'd know if he had something to hide."

Ronni sighed. "He might say no, but he'd never sell us out."

Why, because he's got a crush on you? That's a thin thread to hang our safety on, Ronni.

Daniel slowed the car. He saw no reason to worry the woman, so he kept his thoughts to himself.

"Okay, fine. He won't sell us out, but when will he respond?"

"It's hard to say."

"What does that mean?" The agent spotted a diner with a handful of patrons inside. He pulled up and parked along the street.

"Hard to say. Paul treats time very differently than…uh, the rest of us normal four-dimensional beings."

Daniel laughed. "Come again?"

"It's Paul, so that's as clear as I can get." He could almost hear Ronni shrug.

He narrowed his eyes as he noticed something through the window. "That's promising."

"What?"

"I'm outside the diner, and there's a man with a large bag at a table. It looks like he's selling trinkets. The bag has a classic gray alien head painted on it." He stepped out of the car. "I'm heading inside now."

"I'll try not to distract you," Ronni replied.

The bells jingled above the door as he entered, and a waitress smiled from behind the counter. "Good afternoon."

Daniel took a seat at the counter. "Coffee, please."

"Sure thing, hon."

He inhaled the aroma, already feeling more awake. His eyes widened in surprise when he took a sip. "This is good coffee."

The waitress laughed. "Local. Schuil Coffee out of Grand Rapids."

"If the coffee's this good, it's a great sign for everything else." The agent grinned and glanced at his target.

The skinny man looked up from his burger and smiled. "I knew it!"

"You knew it?"

The stranger stood and walked to Daniel. He extended his hand. "I'm Aiden."

He shook Aiden's hand. "Daniel. I don't follow what you mean."

Aiden pointed toward his bag. "You want a souvenir, right? I told everyone that it didn't matter if we didn't talk much about it. People would still hear and come. I wanted to be on the ground floor. You're probably a reporter, right? You want the scoop?"

The waitress sighed and walked off.

Daniel shrugged. "I'm an accountant for Chevrolet and needed some coffee as a pick-me-up."

Two men at another table looked his way.

One of them snorted. "See, Aiden? I told you. Stop bothering people. We don't want the wrong kind of attention."

Aiden shrugged. "Whatever, Liam. It's like I told you and Jackson earlier—we can't keep this stuff quiet, so we might as well make money off it."

Jackson muttered something under his breath.

So, there are different factions, but it seems most people want to keep it quiet. They are probably spooked by the molecular rearrangement gun and worried about the creepy men in black who might show up. Well, I'm in khakis and a polo, not even a suit.

Daniel picked his coffee up casually and took a sip. "I'm not a reporter, but whatever you're talking about sounds interesting. It's hard not to notice your bag with the alien on it."

Aiden dropped onto the stool next to him. "Look, we made contact with extraterrestrials."

Liam shook his head. "You're a damned fool."

Daniel arched a brow. "Aliens? How do you know it's not an elvish prank?"

"Because elves don't fly around in spaceships." Aiden slammed his fist on the counter. "None of them Oricerans do. I've watched every episode of *Ancient Oriceran History Secrets,* and I've never heard of no spaceships. They don't use that kind of technology."

"Not everybody saw a spaceship," Jackson interjected.

Ah, they want to spill their guts in the end, even if they've decided it's a bad idea.

Daniel smiled behind his coffee cup. "But it sounds like everybody saw something?"

Liam released a long sigh and shrugged. "Some people talk about a portal. Some say a ship with fancy angles and weird symbols. Everyone you ask says something different—except for the light. They all say the same thing about that. A weird light appears, then something happens after that. Some people say it landed and an alien got off and killed a cow. That's what they do, right? Aliens? They mutilate cattle."

A man scoffed openly and rose from a nearby table. "Ain't no such thing as aliens. It's all Oricerans. Everybody knows that. Don't matter if people saw some weird crap. They make it something more because they want the excitement."

He stomped away, followed by his friends. They stopped at the door and gave Daniel the stink-eye.

Definitely members of the silence faction.

An ancient weathered man at a nearby table grabbed his cane and stood, then hobbled to the counter. "I fought in Vietnam. Marine Corps. I saw that thing the other night, and it reminded me of something in Vietnam."

Daniel grinned. "Oorah, brother. I was in the Corps. Daniel." He extended his hand and the old man gave it a surprisingly firm shake.

"I'm Sammy. You ever see anything weird in your service?"

Well, not during my time in the Corps unless you count some Oriceran stuff, but in the CIA...

The agent shrugged. "I was lucky—or unlucky, I guess. I saw nothing weird."

He couldn't help but be impressed that the old man was

still around. Very few Vietnam veterans were left. Maybe magic would help a few more to live longer.

"I was on patrol," the old vet explained, his voice creaky with age. He made a circular motion with his hand. "As the newbie in hell, a lot of them made fun of me. That's why they didn't believe me when I saw it."

"Saw what?"

"Strange lights like everyone here saw the other night." Sammy frowned. "I can't say I saw a ship back then, but I saw the lights."

"And everybody else in your squad?"

"They told me I saw gas or the VC throwing fireworks to mess with me." His eyes hardened. "But I know what I saw. It was the same thing."

Daniel nodded slowly and rubbed his chin. He wasn't sure of the man's age, but even a conservative estimate placed his sighting over sixty years earlier. History was filled with UFO sightings throughout the millennia, but it was hard to separate what might be alien versus merely Oriceran.

"This has me curious. Where did everyone see it?"

Liam and Jackson sighed. Aiden grinned.

Sammy nodded grimly. "The old cow pasture beyond the Thompsons' new house for their son and the mother-in-law. They alerted everyone. A crowd rushed over after that text went out. At the old oak, take a right, go past the blue farmhouse, and look for the pasture on your left. There's nothing to see now, but there was something there."

Why would one faction be so obsessed with keeping this secret? If it was a transient sighting, they could use it for tourism like Aiden wants. Still, the cattle mutilation matches what Ralph mentioned about the weapon. Do they have it or did an alien use it?

Daniel looked at the gathered locals. "So, everyone saw some lights, but people argue about what they saw afterward. You mentioned spaceships, but you also mentioned technology. Did they leave something behind that made it clear they weren't Oricerans?"

Sammy flinched. Jackson and Liam looked down. Even Aiden's smile disappeared.

"I wouldn't know about that," the old vet explained. "I only saw the light."

Daniel looked around and they all shook their heads or shrugged slightly, although their expressions revealed discomfort.

"Thanks. I think I'll check the place out and get some pictures. It'll be a fun story for the office when I get back to Detroit." The waitress was on the other side of the room, so Daniel left enough bills on the counter to pay for his coffee.

No one spoke as he headed out of the diner.

"If they are willing to give the sighting location," Daniel murmured for Ronni's benefit, "it means an alien tech or molecular rearrangement gun won't be there. I'll have to figure that out myself."

Ronni cleared her throat before replying. "Maybe you can run one of the recon drones over the area."

"That's a possibility," he whispered, "but if I show too much odd tech, it might tip them off. These people are far more spooked than I expected. Wait a second. Someone's coming."

A man in a dark suit sprinted down the sidewalk toward him.

Daniel slowed his pace and reached into his jacket for his stun pin. It might be hard to explain the device, but that was preferable to shooting an unarmed man. The stranger slowed and all but stumbled the last few feet.

Sweat covered his brow, and he leaned over to catch his breath. Daniel lowered his hand to his side.

If this guy's Fortis, he's not their best.

"Can I help you?"

"I-I'm Alan Finerman," the man panted.

"Daniel." He waited for a response before adding, "Did you need something, in particular, Alan?"

The newcomer managed to catch his breath and straightened. He adjusted his tie. "I'm with the Aaronstown council."

"And?"

The councilman blinked but didn't look away. "I know what you are."

Daniel narrowed his eyes. "An accountant with Chevrolet?"

"I'm not stupid enough to think only men in dark suits and dark vans will show up. Even the PDA doesn't always dress like that when they deal with paranormal incidents." Alan pointed at Daniel. "You're obviously some sort of Fed."

I'll give the guy credit for good situational awareness.

"You think I'm a Fed?" Daniel nodded toward his rented electric Kia. "Does that look like something they would drive?"

Several more men hurried down the street. From their

casual clothes and frowns, he suspected they were locals rather than deadly agents of a government conspiracy.

Alan drew a deep breath and leaned closer. "I don't care what the others say. I don't want that thing here. It's too dangerous. You'll find it buried in the old corn silo. Get rid of it, please, before someone gets hurt."

One of the newcomers grabbed Alan's arm and yanked him back.

Daniel frowned.

"You best be moving along." The man glared at him to make his point.

The agent shrugged. "I simply stopped for coffee."

"All the more reason to leave, then."

"Fine." Daniel turned and headed toward his car.

"Why did you do that, Alan?" the man whispered a little too loudly as he pushed the councilman farther down the sidewalk. "We have this under control."

By the time the agent opened his car door, the men were out of earshot. He slipped into his seat and slammed the door.

"Ronni, you there?"

A slight crunch sounded over the line. "Yeah," she mumbled. "Sorry, had a mouthful of chips. It sounded like you ran into some trouble."

"Not trouble. I now have confirmation that they have something nasty here." Daniel checked his mirrors to make sure no one seemed inclined to follow him. "All the signs point to a sort of alien molecular rearrangement gun hidden in an old corn silo."

Another crunch followed. "Where's the silo?"

Daniel grunted. "I don't know, and it's too late to ask."

CHAPTER ELEVEN

After thirty minutes, Daniel turned onto a dirt road. It ran parallel to a rotting wooden fence that wouldn't keep a baby in. He pulled the car onto the verge, stopped, and stepped out. A quick hop over the fence brought him into the cow pasture, although he suspected no animals had grazed there in decades.

He was less interested in cows than aliens. There were no scorch marks, flattened vegetation, or debris. Not a single sign of a visitation.

"There's nothing here," Daniel muttered, shaking his head.

"I crosschecked the other data, including the NRO images. They correspond to your location, but the images are nothing more than brief flashes of light. Something did happen there, at least," Ronni informed him.

He frowned as he walked farther into the field. "I don't care about that."

"Don't care about what?"

"The satellite data. I don't need to be convinced that

something happened. These people obviously saw some-thing. What I care about is finding that silo." He glanced around. "I don't see anything like that here, and the coun-cilman was spooked enough that I think I should find it quickly."

Ronni sighed. "There are several silos in the general area according to the aerial images. The closest is a few miles away."

"Close enough to hide something if you're worried it's dangerous." Daniel shook his head. "Well, I'll check those after I inspect the field. For now, I'll walk around and see what I find."

"What about using a drone?"

"No. The townspeople are skittish as is. I don't want anyone to take a shot at me because they think I'm some evil man in black." He strolled through the tall grass and brush that had long since overgrown the field. "Good thing I didn't wear shorts. I'd probably end up covered in ticks."

Ronni laughed. "I have trouble even imagining you in shorts."

"I wear shorts. Sometimes." Something glinted in the sunlight and caught his attention. "What's that?"

"What's what?"

Daniel jogged to the reflection's source and knelt. A small metallic silver-green rod lay in a pile of leaves. A gust of wind must have exposed the item.

"Now what do we have here?"

With its angular lines and metallic sheen it was obvi-ously artificial, but that didn't make it alien. For all he knew, it was a kid's toy.

Daniel picked it up and studied two small grooves on either side.

"I found something," he explained. "I'm not sure if it's random crap someone threw here or alien. It doesn't look old or weathered, though."

He squeezed the two grooves on instinct and the rod twisted and lit up. Several glowing symbols appeared in rows in the air above it. The holographic display paused, the symbols vanished, and more appeared. He couldn't follow the strange symbols quickly enough to see if anything was repeated, but he recognized at least a few of them as stylized versions of symbols he'd seen before.

"Are you okay?" Ronni asked. "I had weird distortion over the line."

"I'm fine." Daniel narrowed his eyes and focused on the device. "I turned it on. My guess is that it's a communication device, especially if it caused interference. Judging by these symbols, it's definitely alien. Too bad I have no idea what they mean."

Ronni gasped. "Wait this means you're in active communication with them. Woah. Doesn't that mean first contact?"

"It's not first contact if we've blown each other up for a while." He chuckled. "Besides, I'm not in active communication with anyone. They're sending messages, but they could all be automated. For all we know, this is the alien equivalent of a four-one-nine scam or Viagra spam."

"I doubt they would use their advanced technology for something like that."

Daniel scoffed. "The DoD spent tons of money and effort to develop ways for networks to survive nuclear wars, and the private sector spent billions to expand it. I'm sure no one thought when they first networked computers that anyone would use the technology to try to sell men erectile dysfunction pills."

Ronni laughed. "Okay, fair point. Maybe they're saying, 'The weather in Michigan is lovely at this time of year.'"

"Could be." He brought the device close to his face. "Hello? Hello?"

The symbols and rate of flow didn't change. If he had been heard, the response remained the same.

"I canna do it, Captain," Daniel said in an exaggerated and poor Scottish accent. "There is no enough power."

"What are you doing?" Ronni asked. "What's with the accent?"

"Giving the aliens my Scottie impression."

"Who's Scottie?"

The agent groaned. "Sometimes you kill me, Ronni. I'm half-convinced you're messing with me." He squeezed the grooves. The rod twisted, and the aerial display vanished. "I hope I didn't inadvertently alert the enemy invasion fleet."

Ronni snorted. "It wouldn't be the invasion fleet. It'd be the space cops."

"Why space cops?"

"You're an intergalactic cell phone thief."

Daniel laughed. "I'm sure they have better things to do, like investigate space murders."

"Anyway, you need to get that back to me ASAP so I can check it out," Ronni ordered. "I'm sure Big Gnome would love a crack at it, too."

Daniel pocketed the rod and headed toward the car.

"Fair enough. I guess the next step is to check out the corn silos. Where's the closest? Hopefully, they didn't try something cute. I don't want to spend all day driving around this county."

"One second." Ten seconds of silence passed. "The closest one is about two miles north. Keep following the dirt road you're on and you'll see it on the side of the road. It's impossible to miss."

"Thanks."

The agent proceeded and spotted an old, rusty silo. He parked and glanced around, but the cracked and decayed wood of the abandoned farmhouse suggested no occupants would be angry or fire buckshot at him.

They came to a place with people, but it's still very rural. I hope this isn't the beginning of some body-snatchers scenario.

He stepped out of the car and made his way to the silo. The rusted door creaked ominously as he stepped inside.

Daniel shook his head. Alan mentioned the townspeople burying the artifact, but it lay in plain sight against a back wall.

"You didn't try very hard, did you?"

It was almost identical to the weapon he'd salvaged in Munich. An artifact of the sky gods: a molecular rearrangement gun.

Is this really something I should take back to the brownstone for Big Gnome and Ronni to mess with? I saw what it could do in Munich. No, some things are better hidden from everyone.

Daniel took a deep breath. He hated the necessity to lie. "There's nothing here."

"Maybe another silo?" Ronni suggested. "They might

have thought the closest place would be too obvious if someone came looking."

"Like a creepy government agent?" He chuckled.

"You're not creepy, although a lot of agents are." Ronni sighed.

"The dirt's been disturbed, and there are a lot of scorch marks," Daniel lied. "I think whatever was here was destroyed. That's probably for the best."

Sorry, Ronni. It's for your own good. You're too curious, and this thing would kill you. It might very well kill me.

"I guess that's better than them having anything dangerous," Ronni agreed.

Daniel chuckled. "Better indeed. I have the communications device, at least. We might not have solved everything, but we collected an alien artifact. At this point, it's too late for Fortis to mess with anything. They'll know someone else was here and will tread carefully, but there's nothing left for them to find."

"Sounds like a win to me."

"Yeah. It does." Daniel pulled his jacket off and wrapped it carefully around the molecular rearrangement gun. "I think I'm done here. We've definitely established that aliens visited here, and maybe we'll be able to talk to them soon with the communicator. It's a waste of time to stay any longer."

"Do you think Fortis has a communicator like the one you found?"

"I don't know. They have more people and have been at this longer, so it's possible." The agent walked to the car. He tried to think good thoughts and made sure not to touch the gun directly with his bare hands. Dying on some abandoned farm in Michigan wasn't on his top-ten list.

Ronni exhaled loudly. "All the more reason for me to figure out how that thing works."

"Yeah. But even if they do have one, we're now on equal communication tech terms with them. Don't worry. I'll see you in a day or two, and you can play with it. For now, though, I'll go dark. It's exhausting having someone always in your ear."

Ronni chuckled. "Sorry."

"Don't be. You've been very helpful. Thanks, Ronni. Talk to you later." He squeezed his ear to turn the comm off.

The agent placed the wrapped artifact in the trunk. Unfortunately, it wasn't something he could check on a commercial flight without special preparations. Those might alert the CIA, and he couldn't risk alien artifacts on a Company flight.

Private charter it is.

Daniel stepped out of the airport with his suitcase and a golf bag, which was the perfect size to conceal the molecular rearrangement gun. He was worried about transporting the dangerous artifact, but it would soon be locked into the vault where it couldn't hurt anyone.

Do these aliens walk around on their planet with thousands of those things? Millions?

The sun was setting, and he already felt more relaxed,

being far from a site where Fortis agents might be. He pushed the thoughts aside and headed home.

As soon as he stepped inside, he spotted a paper plate on a Chef Boyardee pizza box. It held a few pieces of pepperoni—Pops' idea of making dinner. Usually, it meant he felt guilty about something.

Do you feel guilty about keeping secrets, Pops? Maybe you should unburden your soul.

The agent chuckled. He had no right to be mad when other people kept secrets. He lied to so many people about so many things that it was hard to keep track of them all. A spreadsheet of lies might be helpful.

Don't worry, Pops. I'll eat your peace offering once I take care of business.

He set his suitcase by the stairs and made his way to the back with the golf bag. His grandfather wasn't there, since it was his night to hang out with friends at a neighborhood pub. His absence made things easier, at least for tonight. Daniel still wondered if he should ask the old man about what the woman at the black site had said.

Maybe she played me.

As he passed through the comics' room, his gaze snapped to his Batman collection. A newer issue was missing. Tommy, no doubt.

The boy probably wreaks havoc when I'm not here.

Daniel smiled. Neither family troubles nor his recent beating had stripped the innocence of youth from the half-elf. That was something to be protected.

One of the main reasons he had joined the Marine Corps was an urge to protect others. He wasn't sure why it was so strong in him. Maybe his parents' disappearance had flipped a switch. Leaving the Corps to join the CIA and protect people from the shadow threats had been an easy transition.

Still thinking about Tommy, the agent opened the vault and placed the new weapon on the shelf beside the Munich gun. He didn't bother to remove the artifact from the bag. It wouldn't be touched or used ever again.

The one in the corner had already collected a small amount of dust.

This is what started it all. Pops held out on me. For all I know, he came in here an hour later and tested it or something to give a report to that elf he mentioned.

Daniel sighed. As much as it frustrated him, there had to be some good reason why his grandfather had kept things from him. The man had always been cranky, but he cared deeply about his grandson.

After sealing the vault, Daniel made his way up the stairs. He was about to leave the back room but paused to pick up one of the pictures that remained permanently face-down. He stared at his parents' smiling faces. They looked so happy in every picture.

Are you still alive out there, or are you rotting in some Fortis or alien prison?

He set the picture down again but this time left it face-up. They were still alive. Maybe it was wishful thinking, but he wanted to believe that. The Daniel Codex team might bring his parents back to him.

He stepped into the front room as Tommy entered.

The boy smiled. "Hey, you're back, dude." He grinned and nodded at the Chef Boyardee. "And you brought pizza."

"That's something Pops made." Daniel pointed at the boy. "Before I forget, make sure you put that Batman issue back exactly where you found it."

Tommy bobbed his head with a smile. "I always do."

The agent raised a questioning eyebrow.

The boy shrugged. "I always do after you remind me."

"You hungry?" Daniel nodded toward the pizza.

"Sure, dude."

"Let's head up with this pizza. We can crack out a couple of Frescas and share it."

A few hours later, Tommy was asleep on a cot downstairs, but his grandfather hadn't returned yet.

Daniel glanced at a wall clock and frowned.

Where the hell is Pops? It's a little late even for him.

The agent finished brushing his teeth and headed to his bedroom. The old man wouldn't like it if he knew his grandson worried about him, and he'd be grouchy for days if Daniel showed up and embarrassed him in front of his friends.

There's still time before I should call out the troops. And he is a grown-ass man and a veteran.

Daniel frowned as he sat on the edge of the bed and wondered if he should simply go to sleep.

Malcolm had met him at the airport to pick up the alien communications device and take it directly to the brownstone. The Codex liaison hadn't seemed concerned that Daniel had taken a private charter flight home. He'd obviously assumed it was to hide the alien communications device.

That wasn't all I was hiding.

The agent's personal phone buzzed with a text. He snatched it off his nightstand, expecting a message from his grandfather. Instead, he saw a message from an unknown number.

This had better not be Fortis. I'm not in the fucking mood.

Who founded Tripoli? Paul

Daniel narrowed his eyes and stared at the message. Tripoli? Was it a secret question about his last mission there? That had been a couple of years prior, and why would Paul ask about a mission via text message on his personal phone? It hadn't even been a notable operation.

He did, however, know the answer to the question.

The Phoenicians.

The phone buzzed with another text.

How big is the park that holds Gosho Palace?

Daniel blinked. He'd gone on a mission to Kyoto the previous year, so he knew the place. He also knew the answer, but he wasn't sure why.

Two hundred acres.

What type of endangered horse can you find in the Chernobyl Exclusion Zone?

Daniel winced. That hadn't been one of his favorite missions. He'd paired with a GRU team to deal with some unusual terrorists who'd attacked both the US and Russia. They'd established a hideout in the exclusion zone. The entire operation had turned into a giant clusterfuck involving an ambush in which he took a bullet to the shoulder.

Oddly enough, he also knew the answer to the question without thinking.

Przewalski's horse. Why the trivia quiz? Or will this help you with a crossword or something?

That's for you to determine. I want to make sure I work with a certain quality of person before I make life-changing decisions.

Daniel frowned at his phone. A clue had obviously been embedded in the messages, but what? A code? Hidden coordinates?

He shook his head. They weren't random questions and all concerned missions he'd run for the Company.

Shit. Ronni was my primary support on all of them.

She loved to provide fun facts and weird info about mission locations that weren't actionable intelligence. Daniel found them entertaining, but not everyone agreed. She was ordered to stop, and that obedience had probably now become a habit, even though she didn't work for the Company.

What a waste. Stomp out creativity, and you end up with less effective support. In a world of magic and aliens, we need all the damned mental flexibility we can find.

Daniel pulled his Company phone out and brought up the old briefing files related to the missions.

Okay. The common link is her. What about it?

Daniel wasn't about to reference Ronni by name on his personal phone.

Good, Paul texted back. **You understand pattern recognition. Don't worry. I've made sure these messages and responses are secure. You ready to prove yourself in round two?**

Man, this guy sure likes his games. That might get obnoxious later.

Sure.

The questions that followed were about a series of different cities, and each involved one of Daniel's missions. He didn't know all the answers instantly, but with the help of Ronni's files, he was able to figure them out in short order.

He narrowed his eyes. A comet reference for one city, a mysterious fire for another... The final question solidified what Paul was hunting for in Daniel's mind:

What interesting sight was spotted in Basel, Switzerland in 1566?

Spherical objects appearing from the sun. Aliens. Is that your point? That if you take a big-picture view of these things, they all point to possible alien activity?

Daniel waited for several minutes but received no more messages.

Did I pass?

CHAPTER TWELVE

The next morning, Daniel hurried into Nessie's office at the brownstone. Her CIA duties didn't allow her to spend much time there, so he had been surprised when she called him on his Codex phone first thing in the morning to come in for a briefing.

Another alien sighting? Is it UFO convention season?

Her door was already open, so he didn't bother to knock. She sat behind her desk, her hands folded in her lap. An opaque mask lay before her.

Daniel frowned. "What's the big emergency? Fortis? Aliens? None of the above?"

Nessie sighed. "John Rainer."

"What about Captain America?"

She furrowed her brow. "Captain America? What does a comic-book character have to do with John Rainer?"

So, Nessie gets my references, but Ronni doesn't? How does that work?

Daniel stared at her. "Come on. A World War Two hero

ends up in suspension and is resurrected decades later. You don't see the connection?"

"Many strange things happen." Nessie shrugged. "Especially nowadays."

The agent sighed. "Why is he so important? Since you have me here and not Tim, I guess this will involve me shooting someone."

She sighed. "Preferably not, but it might become necessary. As to the importance, we have good reason to believe Fortis intends to vivisect Agent Rainer."

Daniel blinked. "Come again? Why the hell would they want to do that? He's not an alien."

"Even though his regeneration was related to magic, Timothy has information that suggests Fortis is convinced that his 'resurrection' is related to alien technology because of his involvement in certain investigations in World War Two."

She shrugged. "Apparently, because of the identical-DNA-twin woman, they no longer believe that genetic sampling and scans are enough to prove humanity and are ready to take the next step."

Daniel rubbed a hand over his face. "If someone's genetically identical, slicing them open won't prove anything. They won't have a second heart or something."

"I think they're convinced that he can't die and will prove it that way. Unfortunately, the magic that brought him back to life didn't alter him permanently. All they will achieve is to rather painfully kill a loyal American who already gave his life once for his country. It's a travesty, and will gain them nothing to help them protect this country, Oriceran, or Earth." She shook her head. "Timothy got lucky and uncovered Agent Rainer's current location. They are holding him at a black site near the city, which means rescuing him isn't out of the question."

"Is it the one where I talked to the woman?"

"No, unfortunately not. He's held in a far more extensive complex in Arlington." Nessie pointed at the mask. "Do you know what this is?"

"Not the latest fashion trend, I hope. Accessories aren't my style."

It looked like an opaque white mask to him, but he doubted the head of SAD would provide anything that wasn't the result of extensive research and testing.

She pursed her lips. "No. We call it a chameleon mask. We've had a small number of agents test them, and they've proven remarkably useful and stable."

Daniel arched a brow. "Like a chameleon ball? More invisibility?"

Nessie shook her head. "No. It presents a false facial image and voice. It won't fool touch, and probably not magic either, but it'll deceive almost everything else. Sometimes that's all you need to hide your identity."

The agent chuckled. "I hope it lasts longer than five minutes."

"This one should last a good hour or so."

He stared at the mask. "So John's rescue won't involve me going in to transfer him to a different facility with paperwork, will it?"

"No. If Fortis weren't involved, Timothy could have facilitated that himself." The woman took a deep breath and released it slowly. "You will need to raid the place. We also can't be one hundred percent certain who is with

Fortis, and even if they are, if they truly understand what that means."

Daniel frowned. "Meaning what, exactly?"

"We're not them, and we won't kill other CIA agents without good cause simply because they get in the way." Nessie reached under her desk and pulled out a briefcase. "Timothy and I have discussed this. It's a risk to send you in with CIA equipment since they'll know you're an agent, but that's the best chance we have to reduce casualties. Fewer deaths are better on multiple levels."

The agent snorted. "I don't disagree, but how do I raid a guarded CIA black site, rescue a man, and not get anyone, including myself, killed?"

Nessie slid the case over to him. "Immobilization capsules and a stun rod are a good combination as a start." She sighed. "We're not telling you to get yourself killed, only to use the gear to disable instead of kill if possible. I also have a chameleon ball in there that I've tested. It's only stable for five minutes, but that's the best I can do. Use that to get inside, then use the mask so they can't identify you. We have the equipment you need to enter the building as well."

Daniel stared at the briefcase. "This is a big risk, especially for a man we don't know all that well. I don't mean that he deserves what they have in store for him, but we can't rescue him and send him on his merry way. We'll have to bring him in, and that puts our people at risk."

"We can't let them cut a man open because of their ridiculous paranoia." Nessie shook her head. "Our lives are already at risk because others in the CIA have lost sight of what they should be doing, So, no, I'm not worried about risking more to save this man."

Damn, I've never seen Nessie so passionate before. Sometimes I forget she isn't some cool robot who's here to give me toys.

"Fair enough. As long as we're all on the same page." Daniel nodded and picked up the mask and the suitcase. "I assume this is an ASAP rescue?"

Nessie nodded. "Yes. Be aware that for maximum safety, we can't have Ronni back you up. Although we're confident enough under normal circumstances, Fortis might have alien technology that could intercept her transmissions, especially in a fixed facility they control."

Daniel shrugged. "It's not like I always need a babysitter."

"If you're ready, I'll transfer the briefing information to your phone."

He turned toward the door. "Time to save a man."

The agent's outline shimmered as he rushed through the alley to a side exit of the office building. To the public, it was a mixed commercial structure with several different floors rented by various companies. In reality, they were all CIA fronts, with a black-site containment facility in a hidden basement level. Fortunately, it was still an officially CIA-controlled facility, even if Fortis did use it for their own purposes. That meant a few modified ID badges and toys would get him where he needed to be without too much trouble.

You guys should have stuck John in Hangar Twelve if you

wanted him secure. Now, I'll bust him out from right underneath your noses.

Daniel grinned. There was nothing wrong with having a little fun while saving the day.

He paused at the door and studied his surroundings. Depending on the angle, anyone who saw him would only see the rough outline of a nearly translucent human form, but his time was almost up.

It had already taken two minutes to get from his throw-away SUV to this point. He had no delusions that he'd reach the basement before the chameleon ball wore off, but the farther he made it, the less time the agents inside would have to rally and interfere with the mission.

Daniel chuckled and waved the badge over the scanner. The door clicked open, and he hurried in. Nessie's briefing information had been accurate. An elevator was situated at the alley entrance. No one else was around, but he was sure the cameras would pick up the optical distortion of his chameleon ball.

The one advantage he had was that the opposition wouldn't be unmanageable. A black site used by a rogue CIA team would not be fully staffed with guards and elite agents. Fortis might not have to watch themselves as much as his team did, but too much force would cost them the secrecy they craved.

I'm in, but they'll know another CIA agent did this. Talk about spy versus spy.

He marched to the elevator and pressed the Down button, confident that his gloves prevented any finger-prints or DNA samples.

The door opened, and Daniel stepped in. He pressed

the button for the second sublevel, swiped his badge over the scanner, entered the code for the hidden floor, and used his DNA spoofer.

He still wasn't comfortable with how much it resembled a thumb-tip. The techs said the shape was necessary to fool the DNA scanners, but he was half-convinced they were messing with everyone.

I hope the code Timothy gave me works. Otherwise, this will be a very short mission, and I'll have to spend the next few hours avoiding Fortis agents.

Daniel held his breath. The keypad beeped, and the elevator descended. He sighed with relief, but his heart rate sped up when it stopped one floor down.

Shit. What happened? Have they tagged me already?

His optical camouflage was still in place, but they might have thermal sensors in place.

The elevator dinged, and the doors opened. He flattened himself against the side as two suited agents stepped in. He didn't recognize either man.

"Did you hear about Michigan?" one of them asked.

The other shook his head. "What about Michigan?"

"It was supposed to be a quick cover mission or maybe a full clean-up, but it turns out someone had already shown up." The man snorted. "This proves my point. We can't drag our feet if we want to have any chance to contain shit."

"Who showed up?"

The other agent shrugged. "I don't know. He claimed to be an accountant, but it was obviously someone from the government. Maybe PDA or CIA. The higher-ups aren't sure, so we now have a whole fucking town with a credible encounter." He frowned. "There was some evidence that they might have been exposed to alien tech, but none of our guys could find it. If it was there, whoever went in before us has it now."

"Shit."

"Exactly. They're working the disinformation protocols, which should keep it somewhat contained, but fuck, this shit's getting harder and harder —" The agent blinked and tilted his head as he looked directly at Daniel. "What the hell is that? The light's off. It's almost like—wait. I've seen this."

Okay, here we go.

The second frowned in the interloper's direction. "I—shit. It's a chameleon ba—"

Daniel smashed his fist into the man's face as his optical camouflage blurred and became ineffective. The target's head snapped back. His surprised friend wasn't ready for the stun rod shoved into his chest. The device crackled and discharged, and he slumped to the floor.

The first man groaned, and the agent knocked him out with another solid punch before incapacitating the now-drooling second man with a kick.

There we go. Two out. Zero kills.

"Sorry about that." Daniel almost laughed. No one had told him the chameleon mask voice modulator would give him a female British accent. He pulled a phone out to look at the camera. His face looked male.

Okay, thanks for the mismatch.

The elevator dinged, and the door opened to the hidden sublevel. He adjusted his tie before he hurried down a narrow hallway.

Another guard turned the corner, and Daniel jammed the stun rod into his ribs. The man collapsed. An immobilization capsule soon encased him in a polymer web.

The agent chuckled and shook his head. This raid was almost too easy. He strode down the corridor to the containment cell. It was exactly where the briefing information said.

It's nice when the bad guys use CIA buildings that we already have the blueprints for. Thanks, Fortis.

With the help of a code, badge, and DNA spoofer, the door clicked open.

John lay on a cot, his hands behind his head. Bruises covered his face and arms. He sat up and chuckled. "What'll it be this time? Will you beat the shit out of me because I won't admit to being an alien freak? Keep going, pal. You can't make me sing a song when I don't know the words."

Daniel shook his head and pulled his mask up. "I'm here to get you the hell out of this crap hole."

The other man narrowed his eyes. "Wait. You're CIA, and these bastards here are also CIA. What's the deal? Are you a double agent? I won't run off and sing Commie songs if you're a Red. I'll figure my own way out."

He rolled his eyes. "The Soviet Union hasn't been around for a long time, John. I'm loyal to America, but I don't see eye-to-eye with these guys." He nodded toward the door. "We don't have much time. I've immobilized a few agents, but I don't know how many others are on site." He slipped the mask on and ran his finger over an activation pad, and the false face shimmered back into existence. He tapped the side a few times and repeated numbers aloud until he found a male voice.

John furrowed his brow "That's some freaky stuff. Is it magic? I swear, half the crap I see the new agents with all seems like magic."

Daniel shook his head. "No. Very advanced tech, but simply tech."

The other man shrugged. "I don't care what you look or sound like as long as you save me, pal. I guess I owe you twice over now."

They hurried out of the room. Movement caught the agent's attention, and he dragged John around the corner in time to avoid a stun bolt.

"You might as well give up," a voice called. "Reinforcements are already on the way. I don't know who you are, but you did well to get so far undetected. I'll congratulate you on that even if it means a really fucking annoying day for me."

Daniel peeked around the corner and gritted his teeth. He recognized the man: Calvin Cooper. He'd worked with him in the past, but that been a couple of years ago. He remembered him as a solid professional.

John snorted. "It's one guy. If we bum-rush him, we can take him."

He shook his head. "No time, and toys have changed. If you charge in there, you'll be stunned or killed."

Calvin responded with a laugh. "Stunned? Maybe. Killed? No, he won't. He's too valuable. I don't know who you are, but you've already lost, and I doubt you're as valuable as him."

Why does everyone have such nice toys? We don't have time to play around, but if either of us is nailed by that thing, we won't get out of here before his friends show up.

"Why are you helping these people?" Daniel called. "I know you, and you're a good agent. Do you have any idea what they plan to do to John?"

The man inhaled deeply. "Look, we all make sacrifices. He was OSS, assuming the man behind you is even still human, and that's doubtful."

John frowned. "I'm one-hundred-percent human, pal. And what do you mean by sacrifices?" He glanced at Daniel, his expression serious. "What do they plan to do to me?"

"They intend to vivisect you to try to understand your regeneration better."

The other man grimaced. "What the hell? Jesus, Mary, and Joseph, that is fucked up."

Daniel stepped into the hallway, and his hand hovered at his side. If he made a quick movement, the other agent would nail him in an instant. If he could throw an immobilization capsule, he could end the situation without any bloodshed.

Maybe there was another chance, though. Calvin wasn't a bastard like Troy. He could be reasoned with.

He sighed. "This shit is wrong, and you know it, Calvin. Fortis is out of control. They blow towns up and torture loyal agents. That's not what it means to be an American. We're the good guys. You are already fighting a dirty war, and you don't even know if the other side is evil. How can you sleep at night knowing the shit Fortis is doing? Why don't you try to talk to the aliens rather than drop fuel-air explosives on them?"

John clenched his hands. He was more than ready to

deliver a few choice comments via his fists. That was understandable, given their plans for him.

Calvin laughed. "What, you want us to talk?"

Daniel shrugged. "I think it's a good start. It might prevent bloodshed."

"If you're here and you know about Fortis, you know the shit we deal with and the level of technology. It makes half the magic the Oris pull off look like nothing." Calvin shook his head. "It doesn't matter how nice the other guys are. If they're way more advanced, it's only a matter of time before they steamroll us, even if they don't mean to."

"The world isn't zero-sum," Daniel replied. "I don't see why the galaxy would have to be."

Calvin snorted. "This shit won't be like colonization. A bow is much like a gun. At least there was some chance. The guy with a bow could relate to the guy with a gun. But these aliens? No. With the tech they have, we're insects to them. Even if they aren't hostile, they'll squash us as easily as a guy who steps on an ant and doesn't even notice." He grunted. "A few people will suffer so the whole planet survives. Fuck, maybe Oriceran, too. The CIA has always had to make hard choices, and a true patriot understands that."

Daniel narrowed his eyes. "A true patriot doesn't throw away everything great about his country and its values. If you keep this up, you'll be a bigger monster than any of these aliens you're so afraid of."

"Fuck you, asshole. I don't even know who you are."

"It doesn't matter. I'm leaving with John. Get the hell out of my way if you don't want to get hurt."

They locked gazes, neither daring to move. The seconds

ticked by. Daniel jumped to the side and threw an immobilization capsule. Calvin fired his stun rifle, but his bolt flew wide and arced over the metal wall.

The man spun to avoid the capsule, but he'd miscalculated and it struck the rifle.

He released the weapon in an instant and leaned back. The polymer web ejected from the capsule and snared the gun, but the agent's quick move saved him.

Damn. He's as good as I remember.

Daniel yanked a stun rod out and charged. Calvin drew a knife and slashed, intercepting the attack. The stun rod clattered on the floor.

The weapon hadn't even landed before the operative swung the knife again, this time aimed for his adversary's throat.

Daniel ducked the blow and the follow-up thrust. He spun while Calvin was still off-balance and slammed an elbow into the other man's face. A loud crunch accompanied the impact.

Calvin stumbled back, and blood poured from his nose. He made another wild swing, but his foot caught on the polymer web. He fell face-first to the ground, and his knife hand twisted instinctively to block his fall. The hilt impacted the metal floor.

"Shit," Daniel shouted.

John winced. "Damn."

The other agent rolled onto his back and Daniel saw the gash in his neck. "Fuck. Just my luck. The guy who takes me out...is me." He gurgled and coughed blood. "Some Ori should have made a prophecy up about that shit."

I didn't want it to go down this way. I really didn't.

Daniel swallowed and nodded to John. "Let's go. We don't have much time. The reinforcements could be here any second."

The OSS agent shook his head as he looked at Calvin. "Poor bastard."

The next few minutes passed in a blur as instinct and training clicked in. They made it to the SUV without further interference and peeled away from the site. With one last look in his rearview mirror, Daniel spared a thought for the agent he wished he could have saved.

Neither man spoke for ten minutes. "Thanks, pal. It seemed like you knew that guy. I'm sorry it went down like that."

Daniel shrugged. "We'd worked together. He wasn't—" He sighed. "I don't know. You heard him. He believed in what he did. I can't say I agree with him, but it would be nicer if he were simply a psycho who got off on hurting people."

"That's the problem with you twenty-first century types. You don't know how to ignore the obvious crap these guys sell." John shook his head in bemusement. "The thing is, everybody thinks they're the good guys. The damned *Nazis* thought they were the good guys. I get it, but you didn't kill that guy, and it was you or him."

Daniel nodded. "I've rescued you, and in the process, a man was killed. They will want answers. There will be an investigation."

John shrugged. "And given your magic mask, they'll look for the wrong guy. You covered your ass, pal."

"Still, it means they'll be on alert." Daniel frowned. "This time it was one of theirs."

John shrugged. "I'm grateful. You said those bastards planned to cut me up. Even if they didn't, they'd probably use more drugs and beat me senseless while they asked me crap I don't know the answers to. Damn assholes."

Daniel looked at the man's bruises. "Like what?"

"Like Nazi magic rockets, and if they were actually obtained from little green men. I ended up in the sarcophagus before I had done any solid investigation, and the Nazi rockets were why I was sent to Germany. I have nothing to hide." John shrugged. "That wasn't all, though. They focused on a guy I escorted once, a French researcher who was looking into a missing ancient city. It might have had something to do with magic. I didn't ask for the details, since my only concern was getting him from point A to point B."

"French researcher?" Daniel changed lanes. "What was he investigating?"

"He had a theory that the city didn't disappear, but more like...moved. You know...it's in one place one second, and in the next, it's somewhere else. He mentioned something about odd energy readings leaving a kind of electrical trail." John shrugged. "I don't know the details. We were together for only a few weeks and didn't chat much. He was an asshole, to be honest."

The CIA agent nodded. "What was his name?"

"Thomas Bernard."

"It doesn't ring any bells."

Daniel glanced into the rearview mirror. Despite Calvin's talk of reinforcements, they had made their escape before anyone else showed up. That didn't mean, however, that they hadn't picked up a tail.

He made sure to take an indirect route to the brownstone.

John sighed. "So, what happens now? After all, your own guys were ready to cut me up, and I can't exactly hide in this freaky new world."

"I have a team and a safe house." Daniel took a deep breath. "And since we're going there anyway, do you want to help save a couple of worlds?"

CHAPTER THIRTEEN

A few hours later, Daniel sat at the central table in the operations room and stared at the wall. Getting Calvin's death out of his head was hard.

What did I expect? That I'd take on a dangerous group like that and no one would die? Maybe it happened earlier than I expected, but it was probably inevitable.

He shook his head. John was now safe with his team. It would take some time for the OSS agent to adjust, but he might prove a valuable resource. The Codex team needed all the manpower they could muster, and anyone not burdened by working for the modern CIA would be useful for missions.

Yes, the world of the mid-twenty-first century was different than the 1940s, but it didn't mean John couldn't adjust. If anything, given that he'd already known about magic even before he'd ended up in the sarcophagus, it should be easy for him adapt to the modern world.

Daniel released a breath and straightened in his chair. Brooding wouldn't help anything or anyone. He needed to focus on his accomplishments and what else he could potentially achieve, both short- and medium-term.

They'd rescued a man, Ronni and Big Gnome were studying the alien device, and Fortis had no idea who'd raided their black site. Daniel had also ensured that a dangerous alien weapon was now safe and hidden from anyone who might misuse it.

We might not be winning, but we're not exactly losing either. That's progress.

The elevator dinged and the doors opened to reveal Timothy.

The older agent stepped into the room and took a seat.

Daniel looked at him. "Did you just get back from head-quarters?"

His mentor nodded. "Yes. Good work on the Rainer rescue. There's very little chatter about it at the higher levels. Officially, they claim they had a terrorist at the black site, and the cover-up is that his buddies raided the place and rescued him."

The younger man shrugged. "Not all that far from the truth. But they simply pretended John was a terrorist? I get that this is the CIA and not the local sheriff's office, but nothing threw up any red flags?"

Timothy frowned. "Look, the guy's been officially dead for longer than either of us have been alive. There is no documentation, and no publicly stored DNA profile. It was damned easy for them to make him disappear." He blew a breath out and ran a hand over his bald head.

"So as far as they're concerned, a terrorist killed Calvin?"

The older man shrugged. "You didn't kill him, from what you told me."

"At least he'll get recognition for dying in the line of duty." Daniel shook his head and grunted.

"I know that was a tough job, and I hate to do this to you, son, but I need you back on the horse right away for a mission. In fact, I want you to leave first thing tomorrow morning." Timothy frowned. "The only reason I don't want you to leave immediately is that I have to set your cover up."

Daniel frowned. "So, whatever it is…" he gestured vaguely around the room, "it's *our* business?"

Timothy pointed to the holographic globe that spun above the table. "Yes. Alien business. You can slip out of town without the Company knowing. Like I said, I need time to set it up, but it's not a huge problem."

"How?"

The older man indulged an uncharacteristic grin. "By doing what a good field agent does best: lie. As far as they're concerned, you'll meet a new informant with insight into magical terrorist groups."

Daniel nodded. "And what will I actually be doing?"

"Going to a burial site before anyone else interested in aliens hears of it. It's in Baja California, just across the border near Ensenada." Timothy tapped a few commands into a wireless keyboard on the table. The globe display shifted and zoomed in on the area. A small red circle appeared near the border.

"And why would I troll through a burial site in Mexico? What the hell does this have to do with aliens?" Daniel frowned at the display.

"To cut a long story short, a TWA flight between New York and London disappeared without a trace in 1975. It carried over a hundred passengers."

"Planes that crashed into the ocean and weren't found isn't unprecedented in aviation history, recent or otherwise." He shrugged.

Timothy grunted. "That's true, but before this one went down, the pilots reported strange and unusual atmospheric phenomena, including an inexplicable sudden darkness."

Daniel thought for a moment before asking, "What does an Atlantic flight have to do with Baja California? You sure it wasn't a Pacific flight? My guess is that you think you found the passengers, but how can you be sure?"

The older man nodded. "A source passed some information along. At least two of the bodies in the burial site—which is more of an open mass grave, based on reports—match the dental records of passengers from that flight. I assume they all will."

"Wait a second, so someone's already been there?" Daniel frowned. "We're showing up a distant second?"

Timothy shrugged. "Yes, but they only cared about the money they received for the information. We now have the information, and know of the site. The rest of the CIA doesn't, which means Fortis doesn't." The senior agent nodded at the globe. "That also means we can move on this and investigate before anyone else even thinks to try."

"How do you know this wasn't Oriceran mischief? Inexplicable darkness sounds more like a spell than alien technology."

His mentor shook his head. "I have a few Oriceran sources and tried to cross-check. If it involved magic, there should be some magical residue at the site. The gentleman who sold the information already checked that—reliably, I should add. No unusual magic residue." He tapped his forehead. "So—weird activity. No magic. The next most likely reality is that it has something to do with aliens."

The elevator dinged, and both men turned.

Nessie stepped out and nodded a greeting. "I assume Agent Winters has been briefed?"

Timothy nodded. "He's been brought up to speed, yes."

Daniel frowned. "I haven't had a chance to write a report yet, but do you know anything about a scientist named Thomas Bernard?"

The woman drew in a sharp breath and looked away. "No. Should I?"

"John told me about him. Bernard was a researcher he guarded for a while. The man was apparently investigating a city that might have teleported. He mentioned energy readings and an electrical trail. Fortis seemed very interested in it for some reason."

Timothy grunted. "Then they had a good reason to be interested. They have more than enough to keep them busy without worrying about people who have probably been dead for decades, so it must be important to them."

Nessie nodded slowly. "In that case, I need to fetch a little tool. I'd like you to take a few readings with it while you're on this next mission. It might be nothing, but it might be useful. Still, be careful, Daniel. Nothing is what it seems these days, and we have no idea what any of it might mean."

Daniel stepped out of the small VTOL plane. He glanced around the plateau that served as the landing platform.

"Thanks, Jorge."

The grizzled pilot grinned and gave him a thumbs-up. "No, thank *you*, Daniel. It's been a long time since I got to have fun flying under the radar with no GPS or other tracking equipment. Takes me back to my smuggling days. But you know the deal, *amigo*—you have three hours before I'm out of here. The mountains around here ain't safe at night. Not anymore. Between the cartels and all the magicals, people, or critters, it can be dangerous. You never know if you'll run into a motherfucking zombie."

Daniel nodded and wondered briefly why wandering zombies were now a legitimate concern. He grabbed his backpack and strapped it on. "You do what you have to do. I don't think this will take three hours." He slapped a fresh magazine into his pistol. He was prepared for angry coyotes, Fortis agents, and even zombies.

He jogged away from the plane. The site was only a mile away, but the rocky terrain was treacherous. It took him far longer than he'd expected to arrive at the location.

Even as he approached the area, he knew the briefing hadn't been entirely accurate. Timothy had described it as a burial site, but no one had been buried. Instead, scores of bodies littered the ground, neither lined up nor stacked. It was as if they had simply fallen where they stood, like a crowd of people had suddenly died.

Mass execution? But how? I don't see any blood or obvious physical trauma. That means no standard weapons, projectiles, or energy were involved.

An odd reddish hue covered them all. Daniel stepped

closer to one of the corpses. The heavy concentration of corduroy and gaudy prints pointed toward 70s fashion.

He shook his head. "For people who have been dead for over sixty years, you look damned good."

"Don't they, though?"

He spun and raised his gun. Daisy smirked, her hands on her hips. She wore her standard black leather catsuit.

Not exactly the outfit I'd wear to poke around the mountains.

The elf winked. "Calm down, Daniel. Nessie thought you needed a little backup, and I had nothing better to do. If I had known you would point a gun at me I wouldn't have bothered."

Daniel holstered his pistol and nodded toward the bodies. "I don't care if they are in dry mountainous terrain, it's been over sixty years. They should either be decayed or mummified, but other than a strange red tint to their skin, these people look like they died minutes ago. I can't see any obvious physical reason for their death. If they were poisoned or had suffocated I'd expect more signs of a struggle, even if it was an involuntary reflex to something they couldn't control."

Daisy nodded. "I agree. There's no obvious reason these people should be dead."

"Do you sense any magic?" The CIA agent frowned at the nearest body.

She shook her head. "There's a small amount of background magic, but nothing unusual for the area. The bodies themselves don't have any magical residue to speak of." She shrugged. "Whatever happened here, I doubt magic was involved."

Daniel retrieved the multisensor Nessie had given him

and ran the preprogrammed scan. Thankfully, the device didn't require his limited expertise to do its job.

"Do you see anything interesting?" Daisy asked.

"There are some strange readings, based on what Nessie told me I should see. If I'm interpreting this right a massive energy and electrical discharge occurred here, but there's no evidence of that. These victims don't look like people shocked to death. What gives?"

Daisy knelt beside a body. "It could be a side-effect of whatever killed them." She pulled the man's wallet from his pocket, thumbed through it, and held up a driver's license. "Come and take a look."

Daniel hurried over. The license had been issued in 1975, but the man was clearly several years younger in the photo.

"Interesting."

Daisy nodded. "Isn't it, though?"

Searching a half-dozen more bodies revealed similar findings. All victims seemed to be a few years older than Daniel would have expected.

He frowned as he worked through the implications. "We have bodies from a missing plane. They obviously weren't killed on the flight, and somehow ended up clear across the country from the Atlantic." He gestured to the body of a man in a beige suit. "It's as if they all simply fell where they stood. There's no fear or uncertainty on their faces, so this wasn't a mass execution."

"What do you think it means?"

He studied the area, his eyes narrowed. "I think someone snatched the plane and the people and held them somewhere else for a few years. They tried to return the people, but something went wrong." Daniel sighed. "That would explain why they're here, and their facial expressions aren't what you'd expect from people who realize they're about to die."

Things disappeared in Belize, too. Is this how? Alien teleportation tech? My parents were sighted after the initial disappearances, but perhaps the aliens zapped them after that?

Daisy sighed. "But where were they taken?"

"Good question. Away. That's all I can think of."

Daniel considered the remains. There was no reason to return the bodies to Earth if killing people had been the goal. Calvin's rant bubbled up in his mind.

We're insects to them.

He shook his head. Even if Calvin were right, Daniel still didn't agree with Fortis. The difference between a man and an ant was that the ant had no way to communicate with the man. The aliens obviously already understood language, and knew this planet was home to various self-aware species. Perhaps Earth and Oriceran could reach some sort of accord with them.

Maybe.

"I don't think that's the most important question," Daniel murmured.

Daisy looked at him. "What is, then?"

"Does whoever did this understand what they've done?"

She frowned. "Why is that the most important question?"

He frowned at a body as he formulated his response. "Because it's the difference between us having any chance at all, or being ants who simply try to avoid boot heels."

CHAPTER FOURTEEN

Daniel was typing a report at his desk at Langley when Troy Williams sauntered up with a cocky look on his face.

No one looks that happy without it being a problem. I'm not in the mood, Williams. I'm really not in the fucking mood.

"Can I help you?" he asked without looking up.

Maybe if he didn't react, the agent would lose interest and leave. He could only hope so.

"I looked for you the other day, but you were too busy knockin' boots with a new informant." Troy chuckled. "But you're here now, so yay for me, right?"

Daniel saved his work and met the man's gaze. "I'm sure your informants don't like everyone to know their names and faces. It's not like I can invite them for tea and crumpets here at headquarters."

"Just joking." The smile on the other man's face seemed forced. "Look, I need a favor. Now that you're here, anyway."

Daniel looked up at him. "A favor?"

Troy nodded. "Yeah, you know that terrorist chick we picked up? The one from New Veil?"

You mean the alien who knows my grandfather?

"What about her?" Daniel shrugged.

"I need you to come with me. We transferred her here for interrogation, but she's a hard one and won't give anything up. Apparently, you impressed her." Troy snorted.

Daniel frowned. "Impressed her?"

"Yeah. She says she'll only talk to you, so we need you in interrogation. Look, I get that you've got shit to do, but I need you to poke your nose in there and maybe rattle her cage a little." Troy shrugged. "Enough to get her talking, at least. You know how this shit goes. Once the words flow, it's hard for the prisoners to shut up."

Daniel nodded. He hadn't talked to his grandfather about the woman yet, and she probably expected that he had. He also didn't want to pass up the chance for further discussion with a possible alien.

The only problem was that the CIA would monitor the room. Even if Troy weren't Fortis, he wouldn't ignore Daniel chatting with a woman about non-Oriceran extraterrestrials. He needed to make sure he could talk freely without raising suspicion.

"Okay, sure." He stood and straightened his jacket. "But I have to run and get lunch first."

Troy stared at him. "Are you shitting me? I need you to interrogate a terrorist, and you can't do it unless you eat first? And this is after I already had to wait around until you dragged your ass into the office? Unbelievable."

Daniel shrugged and grinned easily. "What's the big hurry,

Williams? You've had her on ice for a while now. It's not like she's going anywhere, and New Veil won't do anything while I buy lunch." He strolled away from his desk. "I'll be back soon."

"You don't take this shit seriously enough, Winters," Troy called to his retreating back. Menace infused his tone. "Someday that'll bite you in the ass. I'd hate to see that. Even with your attitude, everyone knows you're a solid field agent."

Daniel maintained his smile. Troy Williams was the last person on Earth or Oriceran who should complain about someone's attitude.

What's his game? If he is Fortis, why does he want me to talk to an alien? Was Timothy right? Do they want to recruit me? Or maybe he really does think I'll loosen her tongue?

The truth was, none of that mattered. Daniel needed access to the woman anyway. He headed toward the elevator.

Maybe he didn't need lunch before the interrogation, but he did need to borrow a few toys.

An hour later, Daniel found himself seated in a stark interrogation room across from the manacled prisoner. The harsh lighting highlighted her gaunt face and the dark circles beneath her eyes.

Have they even fed her?

Daniel studied her. Fortunately, she lacked the bruises or cuts suggestive of torture, but he doubted Troy Williams would flinch at the idea of inflicting pain.

Troy stood at the back of the room with his arms crossed. "I got him like you asked, so fucking talk."

The woman shook her head. "No. Not with you here. *Especially* not with you."

The agent stormed over to the table and slammed his hand down. "Do you understand where you are, bitch? This isn't some jailhouse. You have no rights here. You can't call the ACLU or a lawyer to save your ass. If I wanted to, I could pull my gun and put a bullet in your terrorist head right now. No one would stop me, and no one would ever know." He smirked. "And if they did find out, they'd probably give me a medal. I want you to think really fucking hard about that."

Daniel kept his face neutral, unsure whether Troy simply wanted to scare the woman or if the other agent harbored a serious intention to execute her. If she were an uncooperative alien, he wouldn't put it past a Fortis member to dispense summary justice. That truth aside, Daniel still couldn't be sure if the man was a member of the rogue CIA group or merely an asshole. His type wasn't all that rare.

The woman gave Troy a blank stare with no trace of fear in her eyes. "If you are going to kill me, do so. Otherwise, leave so I can talk to him."

Troy smirked. "You think it'll be that easy?"

"I think if you want me to talk, you'll leave." She turned her head so she didn't have to look at him.

Troy snorted and backed away. He shook a finger at her. "We're not done here, bitch. Not by a long shot."

He threw the door open, stepped out, and slammed it

behind him. The sound echoed in the bare interrogation room.

Daniel hid a smile.

Time for my little lunchtime surprise.

He reached into his pocket and flipped a hidden switch in the back of an action figure. Thankfully, no one had demanded to check his possessions. He doubted that he could satisfactorily explain to a suspicious fellow agent why he carried a G.I. Joe in his pocket.

Damn it, Ronni, you need to focus on functional concealment of these things. I also don't understand why you're so into all these toys but don't get a single one of my pop culture references.

Daniel cleared his throat. "We can talk freely, but only for a short time. The camera feeds are now spoofed, both audio and visual. This is a huge risk, so make it worth my time before I believe that Agent Williams is right."

The woman leaned forward. The calm vanished and desperation filling her face. "I need your help."

"I know. You told me."

"Did you talk to Peter?" A spark of hope appeared in her eyes.

Daniel shrugged. "Maybe. It doesn't mean I'll tell you. Even if I'm not as angry as some agents, you can't count on that. I have no reason to trust you, and every reason not to. You're still associated with a very odd murder."

"Again, it's not what you think. It was more…an accident." The woman sighed. "I have a different proposal. I need someone I can trust, and you seem less willing to harm me than some of your compatriots. I think we can come to an agreement."

He narrowed his eyes. "Don't get me wrong—if I think

you're a danger to my planet or my country, you'll find me *very* willing to harm you. I'm merely not convinced yet that you're either. You need to convince me you aren't."

She stared at him and swallowed. "I think we can make a deal."

Daniel frowned. "A deal?"

She nodded. "Yes. The only reason we're here is that we're looking for someone, an ally who disappeared. We won't stop until we find him."

"Is that a threat?"

"I'm explaining why it's in your interest to strike a deal." She shrugged. "Besides, you make it sound sinister, but don't you look for your friends and comrades when they go missing?"

Daniel glanced instinctively at one of the cameras. He had no way of verifying if the spoofer was working, but he trusted Ronni. As goofy as most of her designs were, they failed less often than some of the official SAD gear he was issued.

Thanks, Ronni. I probably don't say it enough, but you've been a great help.

"Fine," he muttered. "What kind of deal do you have in mind?"

"We have two humans and an elf we can trade for our ally," she replied.

"And who exactly is 'we?' I'd like to know a little more about who I deal with."

The woman shook her head. "I don't have enough time to answer that, but I think it's a fair deal. Whatever you think is going on, a prisoner exchange is civilized. No one's hurt or harmed. If anything, it's the opposite."

Daniel eyed her in silence for a few seconds. "And who are you trying to locate?"

"He goes by Matteas. Someone must have him captive—I assume some of your people. Otherwise, he would have found a way to signal us already and I wouldn't be here." She frowned and shook her head. "Please. This doesn't have to be more complicated than it already is. When you find him, tell him the prettiest flower on Earth is the iris, and he'll know you can be trusted. After that, he'll know where to go."

They locked eyes, each barely breathing. A good twenty seconds passed before Daniel gave her a curt nod.

"I can't promise anything, but I'll see what I can do. Now, play along." He deactivated the spoofer. "Okay, I've sat here for a while now. You said you wanted to talk to me, so talk. Otherwise, I have better things to do."

I hope they buy this act. I really hope they do.

The woman shook her head. "I changed my mind. Go away." She flicked her hand dismissively.

He shrugged, stood, and adjusted his tie. "Have it your way, then."

Troy waited outside. The man scowled when he shoved the door open and slammed it behind Daniel, who took a moment to enter the lock command before he turned to the other agent with a noncommittal shrug. "She made me sit around, then basically told me to go away. I think she played you."

Troy frowned. "That bitch. She thinks she's so fucking clever."

I hope I didn't sign her death warrant. If they were willing to vivisect John, who knows what they'll do to this woman? And she actually is an alien.

Damn. Whatever I do, I'd better do it fast before Fortis narrows my options.

"What's the plan now?" Daniel asked, nodding toward the door.

Troy waved his question away. "Don't worry about it. I only asked you here because I thought it'd help. I have ways of getting people to talk. Anyway, you have your own work. Thanks anyway." The last words were tinged with bitterness.

Daniel slipped into the office without knocking and closed the door. His mentor looked up from his computer with a frown.

"Don't rush in here like that without knocking or getting my attention," Timothy spat. "You of all people should know that I don't like people to surprise me."

The younger agent activated his silence cube. Timothy nodded and reached into a desk drawer, undoubtedly to trigger one of Ronni's toys.

Daniel was glad he understood. The clock was ticking, and it wasn't an option to wait until they both returned to the brownstone.

Timothy sighed. "Anyway, it's good that you're here. I've poked around here and there about Hangar Twelve. No one seems to suspect you of being there, but if it's not a major alien holding pen, then I still have a full head of hair." He shrugged.

The younger man chuckled. "That's not what brought me here."

"Then what did, son?"

Daniel nodded toward the door. "Troy Williams dragged me down to help interrogate that alien clone or whatever the hell she is." He shrugged. "We had an interesting conversation."

Timothy nodded and set his stress ball aside. "Define 'interesting conversation.'"

"She didn't admit to being an alien exactly, but she said she wanted to make a deal. A prisoner swap, basically."

The older man furrowed his brow. "And what prisoner does she want?"

"Someone named Matteas."

Timothy paled and closed his eyes. He let out a long sigh. "Damn it, of *course* it had to be him."

Daniel dropped into the chair in front of his mentor's desk. "Why? Who is this guy?"

"I've heard the name before. Officially, he's a high-end terrorist leader."

"And unofficially?"

Timothy pointed upward. "He's from up there. Even though they claim they have him under lock and key elsewhere, he's been in Hangar Twelve for a few months. He's their prized prisoner—him and another humanoid who is definitely not from Oriceran."

Daniel nodded slowly. "And what's his deal? This Matteas."

Timothy shrugged. "I don't know. He won't give anything up despite them trying some pretty nasty tricks. I don't know much more than that his people have at least two humans and an elf they're holding. My guess is that's who she wants to swap for Matteas?"

"Yes," Daniel replied.

Timothy shook his head. "It's hard to poke around without them pushing back." He picked his stress ball up and gave it another slow squeeze. "Even if we wanted to do a prisoner swap, I don't know that it's a good idea. There are a lot of unknowns in this."

Two humans and an elf. I wonder who they could be?

Daniel leapt out of his chair. "Two humans. After that shit I saw in Baja, I can easily imagine two people teleported by alien technology while researching an area. Two people from Belize, maybe?"

His mentor sighed. "I know you want to believe that, but it's not your parents."

"Who is it, then?"

"They don't know exactly who the humans and elf are. Genetics are inconclusive, and all the images are vague and indistinct."

Daniel leaned over the desk. "Then it could be them. The pieces fit. The mysterious disappearances fit. My parents—"

Timothy shook his head. "A lot of people have gone missing through the years. Many involve Oriceran, sure, but like you said, you saw what happened in Baja. I wouldn't be surprised if hundreds, if not thousands, of humans have been taken, either willingly or by force. The chance of them being your parents is minuscule, and you shouldn't get your hopes up or do anything if that is the only reason."

"Even if it isn't them, don't we still have a duty to help

those people? I don't care if Matteas is the alien Stalin. Right now, if we want to preserve some sort of peace, incarcerating their important people won't help." Daniel took a deep breath, then fell back into his seat. "Enough incidents can add up to a war even if we don't want one, and we can't win a war with these people, not with the tech they have."

"Presuming we want to go through with this, we'll have to be careful. It's not like we can simply waltz into Hangar Twelve."

Daniel snorted. "Why the hell not? I did before."

Timothy shook his head. "No. You walked up to it, not in."

"I have an artifact—a universal key. It has a limited life, but we can use it."

"As with most things, getting in is the easy part. Getting out, let alone with prisoners, is more difficult." Timothy crossed his arms and furrowed his brow. "I'm not saying no, but we need to be careful how we proceed. If we screw this up, it might not only be our asses on the line, but both Earth and Oriceran too." He nodded decisively. "Talk to Nessie. If we do this, it has to be before they move him or kill him. I only hope this doesn't blow up in our faces."

CHAPTER FIFTEEN

Ronni tilted her head and adjusted her screwdriver. Something was wrong with the coil in her latest device, so she needed to pull the whole thing apart. It wasn't difficult as much as tedious, and she didn't look forward to it.

"Why won't you work?" she whispered. "Why do you have to be so much trouble?"

Her phone rang, and she sighed as she put the screwdriver down.

It was an unknown number.

"Hello?" she answered cautiously.

"I'm outside." The voice was familiar.

Ronni blinked at her phone. "Paul?"

"Yes. Who else would it be?" He sounded genuinely confused.

"You might be surprised. One second." Ronni grabbed a nearby tablet and quickly brought up the external cameras.

Paul stood outside the building with his hands in his pockets. If he were an imposter, they had done a good job of imitating the hacker, including his beard, half-glasses, sensible shoes with white socks, and cargo pants. Several pockets bulged with what were no doubt random goodies. He even wore his trademark combination of a nice sweater over a plain white t-shirt.

Ronni shook her head. No, it wasn't a trick. The man had finally decided to show up.

"I'll be right out." She sighed, hung up, and immediately dialed Daniel.

"What's up, Ronni?" he answered.

She stood and headed toward the elevator. "I wanted to let you know that Paul's outside."

"Outside?" Daniel echoed. "As in, outside the brownstone?"

Ronni blew out a breath. "Yes."

"How did he find the place? I didn't tell him where it was."

"I told you he was good. Finding that kind of information would be easy for him."

Daniel chuckled. "This was a little less cautious than I would have liked. He might be a great hacker, but he could also have been followed if he wasn't careful."

Ronni sighed. "Sorry. I mean, he's a very…unusual guy. This is the way he does things. He's rather like a gun. You point and shoot him at a problem and he'll solve it, but not always the way you would expect."

"Okay, well, I guess this means he's aboard. Show him around, and I'll talk to him later."

Ronni rubbed the back of her neck, nervous at the idea of being the one to introduce him to the place, even though this wasn't her first recruit. "Okay, I'll do that. If you're sure?"

"Yes. I'm sure. Talk to you soon."

Daniel hung up.

She took the elevator to the lobby and opened the door.

He stepped inside and looked around, his expression curious. "I'm ready to go to work on Team… Team what, exactly?"

Ronni shrugged. "We don't have a cool name."

Paul shook his head. "You need to work on that. Labels matter. They can help people concentrate. The other guys have a name. Maybe that's why they're one step ahead of you."

He followed her to the elevator. She pressed the button and cleared her throat. "Um, not that I'm sad to see you here, but aren't you supposed to be at the Company right now?"

"Nope. Well, yes and no." He shrugged.

"Care to clarify? I don't follow."

Paul frowned and remained silent until the doors to the operations room opened. He stepped out and stared at the holographic globe. Big Gnome sat at the table and tapped away at the portable keyboard. Madge sat in a tiny chair near him reading an equally tiny magazine.

"Hey, that's Big Gnome." Paul pointed in amazement.

Big Gnome looked up with a grin. "New recruit?"

Ronni nodded and nibbled her lip. "This is Paul. He's, um, one of the best hackers in the world."

The gnome grinned even wider. "That's what I like to hear. It's not only my own brand I like to help."

Madge set her magazine down and fluttered out of her chair to circle the new arrival. He barely seemed to notice. "Do you need anything in particular?" she asked in her deep voice. "I'm Madge. I'm the office manager here, just so you know."

He shrugged. "I'll let you know, but nothing I can think of right now."

The pixie nodded and flew back to her chair.

Paul pulled out his phone. "I have this for now." He nodded toward the table. "Is this where I should set up?"

Ronni shrugged. "Sure. We'll get you your own office later."

"Good. There isn't enough space here for all the keyboards and monitors I'll need."

Big Gnome looked at him. "How many do you run?"

"Usually four."

"Nice." The gnome scratched his chin. "Maybe I should experiment with four."

Ronni rubbed the back of her neck. "As I was saying, what about the CIA? You're not someone who can make his own schedule there."

"Lunch break." Paul shrugged.

She blinked at the unexpected response. "We kind of do our own thing here. There's no set schedule. You can eat whenever you want."

Paul dropped into a seat a few down from Big Gnome and shook his head. "No. I'm on my lunch break. The Company won't expect me back for another thirty minutes. I'll leave soon, but I wanted an assignment first. To prove myself."

"Daniel runs the field operations. Timothy's in charge

overall, but Daniel coordinates a lot of the mission-type stuff." Ronni shrugged. "You'll meet Tim soon enough."

Paul nodded a few times and scratched his beard. He tapped on his phone. "No reason to wait. Fortis isn't waiting."

A few seconds later, the holographic display changed to Daniel's phone number and ringing sounded through the room speakers.

How did he do that so quickly? I didn't tell him anything about our system.

"Who is this?" Daniel answered.

"Paul."

"I see it'll take me a while to get used to you."

The hacker shrugged. "Most people say that. Ronni says I should ask you about an assignment. If you don't need me, you've wasted your time and mine."

Daniel chuckled. "I have the perfect assignment for you. You'll work with Nessie, Ronni, and Big Gnome, too."

Ronni gasped, surprised that Daniel was ready to bring Paul in immediately on the big mission. She'd only been briefed about it a few hours earlier herself.

The hacker focused on the holographic display. "What's this perfect assignment?"

"I need you to break into one of the most secure places on Earth and help a few unknowns escape without getting caught."

Paul nodded, apparently unfazed. "Oh, you want to break into Level Three-E."

"No. Hangar Twelve."

The hacker snorted. "Only because a bunch of nerds named it."

Daniel laughed. "It's kind of ironic that... You know what, never mind, but yes, there."

Paul looked at Ronni. "To do something useful, I need a real computer."

She hurried to a cabinet at the side of the room, grabbed a laptop, and handed it to him.

He retrieved a strange silver box from his pocket and plugged it into the laptop.

Ronni stared at it for a few seconds. "What's that?"

"It keeps my shit separate from your servers in case something goes wrong. Safer that way."

Daniel grunted over the line. "For whom?"

Paul looked up, his eyebrows raised, but didn't answer.

"Ronni, what he's doing right now?" the agent asked. "What the hell is going on?"

She laughed. "It's okay. He's making sure not to blow anything up."

Paul tapped something into his phone, then started typing on the laptop. Every once in a while, he frowned down at his keyboard as if irritated by the limitation of a single device.

Daniel cleared his throat. "What's going on now?"

"I'm setting this up for you to break into Level Three-E."

"Wait, what? *Now*?"

Ronni slapped a hand to her forehead and rushed to grab a laptop. The agent sounded like he would need extra tactical support, but she wasn't sure she'd be able to help him.

Big Gnome and Madge watched Paul with huge grins on their faces.

The hacker snorted. "Yeah. Why wait? You better get ready. Shit's gonna go down. Doors will open. You'll have to move fast to get in there. I hope you already know exactly who you're looking for."

The agent groaned. "We'll need to work on your team coordination. I wanted something a little less chaotic. Can you delay things?"

The other man sighed. "I already started the procedure. I thought you wanted in there. That was what you said."

"Eventually, not right away."

"Oh." Paul shrugged at the floating phone number above the table. "I can't delay things by much."

"How long?"

He pursed his lips and wiggled his jaw. "Thirty minutes."

Daniel laughed. "I guess I should get ready."

"Yeah, go grab a chameleon ball from Nessie, maybe. You'll need it. Well, if you want to survive. Otherwise, they can take you out. Even then, well... I'll look surprised if they say you're dead, but I'll also look surprised if I run into you as a free man."

"We definitely need to work on your coordination."

Ronni sighed. "He's worth it."

Paul looked at her for a moment and his face reddened. He snapped his focus back to his keyboard and cleared his throat. "Anyway, it won't be as easy next time, even if I have my actual machine and not a borrowed one."

Daniel chuckled. "If this goes well, there won't be a next time. We'll have to do this no-comm for maximum safety in case something goes wrong. Where should I wait?"

"Somewhere out of the way." Paul grunted. "Oh, did I

say thirty minutes? I meant twenty. Sorry. The secondary line of security is a little feistier than I thought. I'll be more careful about that in the future."

"Shit." A rustle came over the line. "Okay. I need to go find Nessie now."

Paul stared at his screen. "Time to stage a break-in."

———

In a darkened unused interrogation room several levels above the target floor, Nessie handed Daniel two chameleon balls and a chameleon mask. "I hope that in the future, we'll plan major operations with a little more lead time."

Daniel snorted. "You and me both."

"Come back to this level when you have him. Timothy, fortunately, already had some things in place for rapid retreat." Nessie handed him another badge and DNA spoofer. "The more we use these, the greater the chance that they'll adapt to it, but they should do for now."

"I know." He shrugged. "But in this case, it will be worth it." He slipped the mask on and activated it. This time the voice matched his gender.

Nessie sighed. "Be careful. If they catch you down there, you'll be lucky if they kill you outright."

Daniel saluted mockingly. "Trust me, I don't intend to get caught."

Ten minutes later, after several flights of stairs and a hacked elevator, he reached the maze of hallways that led to the hidden ultramax and Hangar Twelve. Daniel lingered outside the elevator and waited for something to happen. Anything.

Yeah, Paul may be impressive, but we need to have a serious talk about this shit. In the meantime, I guess I should get into position and wait for his signal, whatever that will be.

The agent activated the first chameleon ball and hurried toward the secured area. At least with Paul at the controls, he wouldn't have to use his joker card. The longer he could keep the thing, the better the chance that it'd help him out of a more serious problem.

He glanced at his watch. It was already later than the timeframe Paul had given. He hurried to the outer prison's massive door.

The minutes ticked by. Daniel gritted his teeth. He'd have to switch to the second chameleon ball soon.

Damn it. Maybe Paul's not all that—

The massive bolts retracted, and a second later shrill alarms sounded.

Time to go.

The agent thrust the door open and blinked. "Oh, shit."

Several prisoners in jumpsuits stepped outside their cells. They looked around for a moment, then rushed toward the exit. The still-invisible Daniel leapt to the side to avoid the criminal stampede.

Damn it. You should have mentioned that, Paul. Fuck.

He looked behind him for a split second. It shouldn't be too bad. After all, they still had to beat all the security. In minutes, everything would lock down.

Wait. The security is probably disabled, which means they can go wherever they want to. Then again, they'll be the focus of attention.

Daniel winked back into existence. An elf with an X-shaped scar on his face stepped out of a cell in the middle and looked at him. He flipped the agent off and ran down the hallway.

Okay. I'll catch his ass later. Even if these guys make it to the upper levels, most of them will get caught. This is a distraction more than a disaster.

He shook his head and continued to Hangar Twelve's massive door. It had already retracted, and aliens rushed out in a stream—at least, he assumed they were aliens, based on their strange living tattoos.

The agent stepped to the side as they rushed forward. "Is Matteas okay?" he called.

A few slowed and eyed him warily.

Daniel held up his hands. "Look, I was sent to get him out. Who do you think was responsible for all this chaos? Most of you won't make it out, but at least he can. I guarantee that."

One of the aliens stared at him for a moment as if trying to decide what to do before he pointed to the corner.

Daniel jogged inside and headed to a huge, well-built man kneeling beside a pale, sweaty man on a cot.

"Matteas?"

The huge man turned. "What?"

"You need to come with me," Daniel shouted. "We don't have a lot of time. We're lucky they haven't already locked this place down. I was sent to get you out."

Matteas frowned. "By who? Maybe this is a trick."

"They said to tell you the prettiest flower on Earth is the iris." Daniel shrugged.

The man shook his head and pointed at the pale man on the cot. "I understand, but I can't leave him. He's in bad shape, and I'm sure they won't treat the prisoners better after all this."

Daniel gritted his teeth. "It's now or never. You might be stuck in this hole forever if you don't leave now."

Matteas scowled and nodded. "Okay, then." He heaved the man over his shoulder. "Let's go."

Shouts resounded through the building as they reached the level on which they were to rendezvous with Nessie and the agent. The alarms continued to wail, and the loud rattle of gunfire and explosions echoed from below and above.

Two agents rushed around the corner and raised their guns but lowered them when they saw only Daniel. Matteas and his sick comrade were currently masked by the chameleon ball, but they were running out of time.

I'm impressed it still works when you're carrying someone.

Daniel nodded to the stairwell. "They need reinforcements one level up. Some elf assassin has gone berserk. They sent me to check on something."

The agents exchanged a glance, nodded, and rushed toward the stairwell.

The operative continued down the hall, and after a few turns, he located Nessie.

The woman opened her briefcase and pulled out several more chameleon balls. She tilted her head when she noticed the distortion that defined Matteas.

"I take it you got him?" Nessie asked.

Daniel nodded. "Yes."

Matteas grunted and his shape shimmered briefly. "Will you help us escape too?"

"Yes. We don't have much time. Most of the prisoners have already been contained, and they're well aware that Matteas has escaped. The alerts have marked him as the highest-priority recapture." She released a sharp breath. "They've managed to lock down the elevators completely, so you'll need to use the stairs. The additional chameleon balls should get you to the secure garage. I've made arrangements for you to borrow a vehicle that you must destroy later to remove any evidence."

Daniel glanced down the hall. No additional agents were in sight, but loud noises still indicated a sizable response team. "Which vehicle?"

She looked down for a moment and sighed. "Find parking spot fifty-two. If I suddenly disappear, it'll be too suspicious.' She handed him a key fob. "Once you've escaped, use program Z-twenty-one. Go ahead and activate program Z-twenty-two from the console after you're out and away. You'll have two minutes to clear the vehicle before it destroys itself. That is the best way to leave no potential evidence behind."

Matteas' optical camouflage failed, and Nessie handed him two new chameleon balls.

"Besides the potential of treason, this escape will cost the CIA millions of dollars." She gave Daniel a new chameleon ball as well. "Good luck. I hope this is worth it in the end."

The agent nodded. "Thanks, Nessie."

Matteas adjusted the sick and unconscious man on his

shoulder and looked from one agent to the other. "What are you getting out of all of this?"

"Supposedly, the return of two humans and an elf."

The huge man nodded. "Fair enough. We should go."

Daniel snorted. "Yeah, we should. Save the gadgets until we really need them."

They headed out and turned toward the stairwell opposite the one they'd taken to that floor.

The agent slowed as he closed on a room he recognized —the same interrogation room where he'd visited with the woman. The door was slightly ajar, and a soft groan came from inside.

It can't be.

Matteas snorted. "We don't have time to stop. If I don't make it out of here, you won't get your people back, either."

Daniel shook his head. "You don't understand. One of your people was in there the last time I saw her. The one who told me about the irises." He threw the door open.

She lay on the ground, and bruises and burns covered her body. Heavy track marks on her arms suggested she'd received more than a few rough injections. She was pale, and one eye had swollen shut. Reddened bandages covered weeping wounds.

Matteas narrowed his eyes. "Those bastards."

He stared down at the woman, a deep frown on his face.

This was your plan, Williams? Torture her to death because she won't answer your questions? What good is it if we become monsters? You might start a war trying to stop one.

Daniel hurried over and picked the woman up. She was

mercifully light, considering they had to run up several more flights of stairs. "Let's get going."

———

The alarms still blared as they stepped out of the stairwell into the secure garage. A few feet in, the chameleon balls failed, and they all winked into existence.

Daniel hissed. "Shit, but I guess it doesn't matter. We're here."

He was grateful for his chameleon mask. He wasn't sure if Paul and Ronni still controlled the cameras, but he hoped he wouldn't return to the CIA and end up locked up in a small room with Troy Williams. All he needed was for that asshole to kick the crap out of him and ask questions about aliens.

They ran through the rows of cars, looking for the vehicle. Forty-nine, fifty, fifty-one…

A rather nondescript gray van was parked in space fifty-two.

"This is it." He put the woman gently on the ground and used the key fob to unlock the vehicle.

Matteas laid the sick man in the cargo area and the woman in the back seat as Daniel slid behind the wheel.

The agent turned on the engine and waited for the huge alien to drop into the passenger seat. The van screeched out of the parking spot and accelerated toward the closed gate.

"Normally getting out of the secure garage requires more than a few codes, but my guess is that she has set that up for us." Daniel tapped the console until he brought up a custom program menu. There were only two options: Z-twenty-one and Z-twenty-two. He tapped the first.

The massive doors to the garage rumbled open, and his heart thundered as he slowed to allow the gap to widen enough to drive the van through. He floored it and the vehicle screamed up the ramp.

Daniel checked his mirrors constantly. No one seemed to be in pursuit, but he couldn't be sure if anyone had seen them. The escape depended on Paul and Nessie overriding the normal security measures. They'd accomplished something very difficult on a tight timeframe, which would make it obvious that it was an inside job. What had merely been extremely difficult now would be almost impossible in the future.

The CIA would review their security measures and tighten them. They would probably also move the prisoners to a different facility.

Matteas mentioned a highway exit near the Virginia border. Daniel had tried to talk to him a few times, but the man ignored him and simply scowled out the window.

The agent glanced into the back seat. The woman was conscious but remained silent.

I don't know if I did something worthwhile or made a horrible mistake. Or did I do this only because I think they might return my parents?

He frowned, honestly unsure of his own motives.

The exit appeared. Daniel took it and maneuvered the van onto a side road. "What now?"

"Take the next right and continue until you see an abandoned farmhouse."

The agent snorted. "What is it with you people and farms?"

Matteas gave him a quizzical look but shrugged in response.

Ten minutes later, they took a dirt road that led to the abandoned farmhouse. Nature had long since taken over the building, so now it was little more than a pile of wood.

"We're here," Daniel murmured. For the first time since leaving CIA headquarters, his heart rate slowed.

Matteas opened his door and stepped out. "You help her. I'll get the other one."

The operative nodded and opened the back door to help the woman out. Once out of the vehicle, she pushed away from him and limped on her own, shaking her head.

The alien appeared with the sick man in his arms.

Daniel took a deep breath. "What now? Will you signal someone? Neither of you has any tech on you."

The woman winced and nodded. "We have our ways. There was a reason he asked you to come here." She took a deep breath, still clearly in pain but surprisingly mobile given her condition.

Daniel shrugged. "A deal's a deal. This is supposed to be a prisoner swap. Very civilized, I believe you said."

His stomach knotted, and his heart thudded. Now that they were away from headquarters, the aliens might kill him. He couldn't believe he hadn't considered that before. Death by molecular rearrangement seemed frighteningly real.

The woman looked at Matteas and he gave her a curt nod.

"Yes," she whispered. "A deal is a deal. We'll bring your people now."

Daniel breathed slowly and deeply, his chest tight.

They might be returned to me very soon. Still, maybe it isn't Mom and Dad. I have to remember that.

An oppressive silence smothered the area before an inky sphere of darkness materialized a few yards away from them.

They have no obvious device. Interesting. I wonder how they pulled that off.

The sphere grew, flattened, and lowered itself to the ground, where it expanded into a pool of deep darkness. The entire area dimmed as if the blackness were hungry for light and sucked it in. The bright day became twilight in mere seconds.

Sudden inexplicable darkness, huh?

Dark particles flowed from the pool and coalesced into humanoid shapes. Daniel squinted and tried to make out who it was. His pulse pounded in his ears.

Three adult forms, one slightly smaller than the other two, appeared. They moved closer, until he could make out their features.

Two human men and a Light Elf stepped forward.

Daniel recognized none of them. His heart sank.

A moment later, a small form rushed from the pool. What appeared to be a ten-year-old boy looked around, wild-eyed.

"Are we back home?" he asked.

The alien woman grimaced. "What is this? It's not what we agreed to."

Daniel shrugged and tried to hide his disappointment. "It's not like I control your strange portal."

She shook her head. "You can't have them all. That wasn't the deal."

Matteas glared at her. "Quiet."

She sighed and looked away.

The aliens stepped past the arrivals and their forms receded into the dark pool. After a few seconds nothing remained of the three aliens, and the shadows vanished.

Normal daylight returned, leaving Daniel alone with the abductees.

He smiled at the group. "Welcome back to Earth."

One of the returnees was an older Caucasian man in an expensive Armani suit. The other was a Chinese man barely out of his teens, and judging by the Mao suit he wore, he'd probably been snatched long before.

The latter rattled something off in what might have been Mandarin. Daniel grabbed his phone and brought up a translation app. He didn't know any Chinese dialects.

"Say that again."

The man repeated himself more slowly. The phone translated in a natural-sounding English voice, "Where am I?"

The agent spoke into the phone and let it translate. "The United States of America."

The man sighed. "Can I go back to China soon?"

Daniel shook his head. "Probably not. Sorry."

He sighed again and fixed his gaze on his feet.

Trust me. I know how you must feel.

The elf frowned. "I shouldn't be on Earth. I'm not authorized for this." He eyed Daniel warily. "Are you a Silver Griffin? I want you to know that I didn't violate the rules willingly."

The boy stood quietly, his eyes still wide with awe.

The agent sighed and asked the elf, "What's your name?"

"Yarvin."

"You've been out of circulation for a while. Don't worry. Elves move openly on Earth now."

He blinked in surprise. "Excuse me?"

Daniel shrugged. "A lot of things have changed, but I can take you all to a safe place."

The boy looked at him. "Who are you?"

"A friend. You can call me Daniel. Welcome home."

CHAPTER SIXTEEN

Nessie shook her head as Daniel walked into the operations room with the odd group of refugees. Yarvin, Chen, and the Caucasian man, Kevin, still seemed a little shell-shocked. The boy couldn't remember his name, but that might have been the result of abduction trauma.

The adults had experienced memory loss as well, but less than the kid. They seemed content to follow directions quietly, which was a relief. Daniel didn't want to interrogate them yet, but their questions might have made that necessary.

"Malcolm's taking the van across town to self-destruct," Daniel explained to Nessie. "It looks like a clean operation."

She nodded and studied the four new arrivals.

The returnees stared at the holographic globe over the main table. On the way over, Daniel had told them the current year. Chen had been taken during the 1960s, Yarvin in the early 2000s, and Kevin only a couple of years before. The boy couldn't remember anything from before he'd been taken.

Chen didn't seem amazed that magicals now lived openly on Earth, but perhaps returning after an alien abduction trumped anything else in terms of surprise.

Daniel gave Nessie the rundown. She seemed more annoyed than impressed.

"A failure of imagination," she muttered.

"Excuse me?"

She nodded to the returnees. "I think we all assumed these people would be recent abductees. Of course, all the available evidence we had indicated that might not be the case, especially given what you found on your little Baja jaunt." She chuckled. "Well, it seems we're a modern-day underground railroad for the weird and unexplained. There are worse things."

Kevin stepped forward. "I get that we can't simply go back immediately. Daniel explained what might happen with either the aliens or the government. I hope you'll give us some time to settle in. I don't think I can deal with a ton of questions right now."

Nessie sighed. "Indeed. But don't worry. You're safe, and we'll give you all the time you need. You can stay here until we make better arrangements."

Kevin and Yarvin nodded. Chen did too, once someone translated.

Daniel allowed himself to smile. He wouldn't lie to himself and pretend he wasn't disappointed that his parents hadn't returned, but he'd helped save four people. Not a bad day's work.

Nessie turned to Daniel. "You need to go home now."

He blinked. "Huh? Why?"

"We need you to be where you're supposed to be." She

pointed to herself. "I'm background noise and easy to ignore, like wallpaper. They don't watch me, but they do watch you. If they can't find you after today's episode, it will raise questions we don't want to answer. Our efforts made it seem that you left headquarters twenty minutes before the incident occurred. Some agents actually did leave around that time, so it will seem reasonable, but get going before they have a legitimate reason to suspect you."

Daniel nodded. "Okay, fine by me. I have a game tonight anyway, and after today, I deserve to relax a little." He nodded to the returnees. "My people will take care of you. I promise."

The boy rushed over and wrapped his arms around the agent's legs. "I want to go with you."

He chuckled and ruffled the kid's hair. "Right now, we need to keep you safe and away from the bad guys. Understand?"

"Will you come back?"

The agent nodded. "Yes, I will." He extricated himself and headed toward the elevator, but stopped at the table and looked at Ronni. "Where's Paul?"

"He went back to work a long time ago." She shrugged. "He actually showed up after they shut the alarms off and acted confused about why he couldn't get back inside since he had finished lunch."

Daniel chuckled. "He might make a good field agent if he can lie to a bunch of people at the CIA and not get caught." He frowned. "But we still need to have a discussion about plans. We accomplished what we needed to, but a better strategy would not involve flooding headquarters with dangerous criminals and magicals."

Ronni winced. "He's the best hacker around but is very literal about orders sometimes. Okay, almost all the time. Paul does the job but doesn't always think through all the implications."

The agent ran a hand through his hair to curb his irritation. "I'll keep that in mind next time, but I will admit that what he pulled off was very impressive, especially given the timeframe."

She smiled. "I told you he was worth it."

He leaned in to whisper, "You know he has a thing for you, right?"

Her cheeks reddened. "Yeah, I know."

I won't tease her by asking her if she has a thing for him, but it's very likely.

Daniel glanced quickly at the glum-looking boy. He felt for the kid, but if he took him home, Fortis would probably have him dissected by the next day.

Time to go act like I didn't turn the CIA on its head.

***

Daniel sat back and smiled as Connor gathered his miniatures. They'd gone over loot and possible purchases rather than spend much time adventuring, but with the current campaign concluded, that was to be expected.

We kicked a lot of Drow ass. I wonder what he has cooked up for us aboveground?

The DM picked up his third Joe Blow of the night and took a sip. He frowned. "Too much vodka, not enough Fresca."

Daniel nodded. "That's not something the average person will ever hear in their life."

Connor shrugged. "What can I say, I'm full of surprises. Aren't we all?" He winked.

The agent almost laughed. The game had made it easy for him to act like he hadn't seen Connor at work. His friend did the same. Everyone loved being in on a secret, after all.

If anything, the fact that his friend now knew the truth lowered the tension Daniel usually felt during game night. Connor was one less person he had to lie to.

There's probably something useful I can do with that.

The DM placed all the miniatures in a box and grinned. "I thought about how you all challenged my honor last time."

Juan chuckled. "'Challenged your honor?'"

Taylor and Lorelei looked up from their character sheets with curious expressions.

Connor pulled five crisp one-dollar bills from his wallet. "I think it's time for another For Want of a Dollar challenge, lightning edition. We play with different challenges for each bet until the competitors run out of money."

Everyone grinned and grabbed their wallets. When they had their money ready, the agent asked, "Well, what's the first bet?"

The challenger rubbed his chin. "We're all pretty drunk."

"I'm trashed." Juan giggled.

Lorelei shrugged. "I don't know if I'd say I'm *pretty* drunk, but I am drunk."

Daniel and Taylor exchanged glances.

Connor stood. "With the miniatures and dice put away, I think we should all stand on our heads."

Juan barked out a laugh. "Are you serious, man? We're not little kids."

The DM grinned. "Unless you're too afraid to face me." He waved a dollar above his head. "Fear me and my glorious headstand ability."

Daniel snickered. His friend might have had a few pre-game drinks before he'd started in on his Fresca concoctions by the looks of it.

"I'm game." Taylor stood, and Juan and Lorelei joined him.

"Everyone, get ready," Connor shouted. He leaned forward and lowered his arms. "And go!"

Taylor and Juan failed immediately, but Lorelei held on for a few more seconds.

Daniel didn't have much trouble. Given the reality of his day job, he didn't ever risk being drunk. He'd simply pretended to down the booze, but he didn't mind Connor having a little victory. He allowed himself to fall next.

The DM dropped to the floor and stood with a grin. "Easy money."

"Okay, John Connor."

His friend looked at him. "Huh?"

"*Terminator 2: Judgement Day.* It's a classic."

Connor shook his head. "I'm way too drunk to remember quotes from nearly-fifty-year-old movies." He burped.

"No respect for cinema history." Daniel smirked. "Okay, what's the next bet? We should all pick one."

Juan nodded. "I want to go next." He pointed to several empty cans. "Let's juggle three cans."

"None of us can juggle," Taylor pointed out.

"Then it won't last long."

They collected their three empty cans with stupid grins on their face and exchanged looks.

Juan smiled. "Three…two…one."

Daniel's extensive experience with exotic or magical gadgets and weapons and Marine and CIA training were no help at all. It appeared that dexterity in the field had little benefit in his current challenge. The only reason he wasn't the first out was his relative sobriety, although he lasted only a few seconds longer than Juan, Taylor, and Lorelei. This time Connor won on skill alone.

"Did I ever tell you about how I wanted to join Cirque du Soleil?" he asked as he juggled the cans.

"Yes," the other three shouted in unison, and Daniel chuckled.

"You tell that story at least half the time when you're drunk." He shook his head. "Let's move on."

***

After several bets, the casualties mounted. Juan ran out of money first. Lorelei and Taylor went out on the same round. Daniel hung on and had a few victories but was soon down to a single dollar thanks to Connor's ridiculous luck.

The DM cackled. "Time to finish this farce."

"It's my turn."

"You think you can beat me?" Connor gestured with his fingers to bring it on. "Do it, shopkeep. Show me what for."

The agent considered his choices for a long moment before announcing, "Breath-holding."

The other three clapped.

Connor grinned. "You're on." He stood and shook out his arms. "I'm ready when you are."

Daniel took a deep breath. "One…two…three."

The men inhaled a breath and stared at each other with their mouths closed as their faces gradually reddened. The seconds ticked away as their friends cheered them on.

Daniel's lungs burned, but he remained determined. Connor looked like a desperate man about to perform a HALO drop into a terrorist stronghold.

Another thirty seconds passed, then another sixty.

A quiet hush fell, and the men still locked gazes, although both began to shake.

Connor dropped to the floor.

Daniel gasped and gulped in much-needed air. After a few seconds, he rushed to his friend's side.

The DM sat up with a grin and drew in a long, deep breath. "Didn't hear me breathe before that, did you?"

The other three blinked in surprise.

Daniel snorted. "You pretended to pass out?"

"Ain't no true honor in For Want of a Dollar except victory." Connor held out his hand. "And tonight's my night."

The agent handed over the dollar and a few seconds later, burst into laughter.

An hour later, Connor was the last person left. He hadn't even called for his ride yet.

Daniel retreated into his bedroom and returned with his silence cube.

Connor frowned. "You sure you want to play with that here?"

"I'm sober. Hell, even *you* are decently sober at this point."

"It's not my fault you're short on vodka." He stared at the cube. "Seriously, though, what's this about?"

The agent leaned forward with a grin. "It *is* your night, Connor."

"Yeah, I know. I won all those bets."

Daniel shook his head. "That's not what I mean. The thing is, you know what I really do now. As part of that, I spend a lot of time recruiting skilled people for something even more secret than the CIA. I get pissed when I see talented people treated like crap simply because they've found the truth."

Connor blinked. "What are you talking about?"

Daniel glanced around, but it was a reflex gesture. Pops always came home late on games night.

"Let me ask you, Connor—do you want to spend the rest of your life with CIA dicks who think you're a laughingstock or do you want to save the worlds?"

"What the hell are you talking about?"

"I'm part of a group that's involved in an unusual project, and we could use an analyst. Let me tell you a little something about aliens."

CHAPTER SEVENTEEN

D aniel sighed contentedly as he downed coffee from the Green Lantern mug. Yesterday had been satisfying, with the end of a game campaign, leveling up of characters, and a new recruit for the team—not to mention breaking into an ultra-secret CIA prison.

I am damned good, aren't I?

While a few of the escaped and dangerous magicals remained free, it was hard not to be proud that he'd accomplished something nearly impossible.

Tommy smiled as he leaned against the counter. He glanced toward the apartment stairs at the sound of steps squeaking. Pops descended in his unfastened robe.

The boy laughed and covered his eyes. "You're gonna traumatize me with your old-man junk, dude. Put that thing away."

Peter snorted and tied the belt. "Whatever, boy. You simply don't like staring into your future."

Daniel chuckled.

His grandfather's expression softened. "I bought too

much of my Quaker Oat Squares cereal the other day at the corner grocery. Do you two want some?"

Tommy nodded. "Sure thing, Mr. Rooney."

The agent shrugged. "I planned to stop off at the Lox and Key to get a bagel, but I might as well have cereal instead."

Peter nodded toward the stairs. "Follow me, then. I won't bring all that nonsense downstairs."

A few minutes later, they all sat at the tiny dining room table and devoured their breakfast.

The old man swallowed. "You're not bad, Tommy, for someone whose brain must overheat because of all that hair."

Daniel shook his head, a little concerned that the half-elf would take offense.

Tommy whipped his hair back and forth. "You're jealous because you can't do that. You know you love it."

"If I did that I'd probably knock myself out." Peter shrugged.

The boy looked at Daniel. "You should grow your hair."

"Me?" Both Daniel and Peter snickered.

Tommy nodded. "Yeah. You have your own shop, so it's not like your boss can complain about your long hair."

Long hair makes it difficult to use decent disguises and specialty equipment. And I doubt Tim would appreciate it if I showed up with long locks when he has none.

Daniel shrugged. "When I go to acquire artifacts, people often have a certain expectation of the kind of man they'll meet. They won't imagine the long-haired kind, but maybe I'll try it in the future." He ran a hand over his hair. "Plus, my years in the Corps may have permanently imprinted me with the idea that long hair is bad."

Tommy shrugged. "Your hair." He continued eating.

Peter nodded, a thoughtful expression on his face. "A lot of nonsense from my time in the Army stuck with me, too."

The agent glanced at his grandfather. The old man had seen action in both Afghanistan and Iraq but had chosen not to be a lifer and left to open his oddities and antiquities shop instead. He didn't like to talk about his time in the service, and Daniel always respected that. Not everyone liked to recall situations where they'd had to kill, whether it had been part of their duty or to protect themselves.

His grandfather shook his head and glared at him. "And don't think I haven't noticed how much Fresca is missing after your barbarian horde raided the apartment last night. Savages, nothing but savages."

"I'll pick some up on the way home from work. The way you act, it's like you think the special Fresca spring will run dry any day now."

Tommy laughed. "I bet they have something like that on Oriceran. The Glorious Spring of Eternal Fresca."

Peter leaned back, and his eyes lit up with pure wonder for a second before he scowled.

Daniel snorted. "We'll keep an eye out for a Fresca-related artifact."

His grandfather shrugged. "Nothing wrong with a quality grapefruit-flavored drink."

The half-elf laughed cheekily. "Dude, you are so *old*."

"True quality is wasted on the young." Peter stood and walked into the kitchen. A moment later, he returned with three cans of his beloved elixir and set one in front of each of his companions. "Drink enough of it and you'll appreciate it."

The agent glanced dubiously at the can. "Maybe it's an acquired taste."

His grandfather sniggered. "No. An acquired taste is what someone says when something tastes like crap. Fresca is good."

Tommy shot out of his seat. "That's what I say, dude!"

Daniel chuckled and shook his head. His grandfather was a good man, but he was also stingy and had distinct habits—patterns he'd violated in multiple ways that morning.

"What's the occasion, Pops?"

Peter shrugged. "Just felt like it."

Years of intelligence work had taught Daniel a very important lesson. Whenever habits or patterns changed something had happened, and usually something huge.

He popped the top of his can and drank thoughtfully. The sweet flavor played over his tongue.

He's in a real good mood, but why? What changed?

Daniel kept his expression neutral when he remembered what the alien woman had first said to him.

Ask Peter. He'll know.

He set the can down and watched his grandfather shake his finger at Tommy as he expounded on the degeneration of modern soft drinks.

Does he know about the breakout? If he and that alien woman are friends, he might be glad she escaped.

She might be gone now, but that doesn't alter the fact that she asked for him.

Just who the hell is *Pops?*

An hour later, the agent sat at the operations table and chuckled. When Big Gnome and Ronni had set the holographic projector up, he doubted either of them had expected it to be used by a kid to watch cartoons.

"How are you doing?" he asked the boy.

He glanced briefly at Daniel. "Doing good. That nice Mrs. Nessie gave me a name because I can't remember mine."

"Her name actually isn't— You know what, don't worry about it. What name did she give you?"

"Jake."

Daniel nodded. "That's a nice name."

"She also says she can't find my parents and doesn't know if they're even still around. Something about DNA?"

"We'll make sure you're taken care of." He smiled reassuringly.

Nessie had taken DNA samples from all the returnees. She hadn't found a match in any DNA database, but depending on when the boy had been taken, there might not be any record of him. His lack of knowledge about modern technology might be trauma-related, but it could also mean he'd been abducted decades before DNA scans were common.

Chen had no desire to burden his family, and Yarvin and Kevin were both reluctant to reintegrate into society right away. They wanted to be sure that neither strange CIA factions nor aliens would murder them in their sleep before they attempted that. The now-open interaction between Oriceran and Earth seemed to bother the elf less than his kidnapping by aliens and subsequent memory loss.

Jake shrugged. "It's okay. Everyone's been very nice, and Big Gnome made me a cool toy."

The boy held up a little wooden man with a handle on the back. He set it on the table and turned the screw several times. The figure took a few uneven steps forward before a techno tune started and the toy began break-dancing.

Daniel chuckled. "That is pretty cool."

Jake quickly shifted his focus from the toy. "I don't remember a lot of stuff, not even my family. Will I ever remember them?"

"We'll figure it out." Daniel smiled gently. "Do you remember anything about where you were?"

The boy nodded. "A city, but there were trees and stuff too. They didn't look all that weird."

Daniel frowned and listened intently. "And the beings who took you?"

"All the ones I saw looked like us, but sometimes they had funny pictures on them." Jake shrugged.

The tattoos. What do they mean? Are they humanoid, or is that just a shape they use for infiltration and study?

Jake blinked several times and wrinkled his face in concentration. "I remembered something. Someone told me to say something when I got here. I was supposed to tell it to whoever found me."

The agent's heart thundered. "What?"

Jake furrowed his brow, thinking hard. "I was supposed to say 'Tim Franklin,' and then two other things."

The likelihood of some kid abducted by aliens showing up by chance with his mentor's name was astronomically low.

Daniel swallowed and maintained a neutral expression. "What else were you supposed to say?"

"Uh, 'Winters,' and…'CIA.'" Jake shrugged. "They said I must say that stuff and tell whoever found me the plan worked. I…" He sighed.

Daniel stood, his heart racing. "What plan?"

Jake shook his head. "I don't know. I didn't even see who told me. There was only a voice, but they said it was very important. They sounded worried."

The agent forced a smile despite feeling like he'd been sucker-punched "Don't worry about it. I'm sure we'll figure it out."

Jake nodded but still looked anxious.

Ronni strolled in and smiled at them. "Hi, guys."

Daniel nodded a greeting. "I better get to the Company. After what happened the other day, they'll be suspicious of people who spend too much time out of the office." He winked at Jake. "I'll be back later."

The boy beamed happily, his worry vanishing in an instant. "Okay, Daniel."

Time to go to work and get some answers, no matter what. I'm tired of people keeping shit from me.

Daniel was halfway to headquarters in the Jaguar when Nessie called on his Company phone.

He answered on speakerphone. The entire inside of the Jaguar was equipped with anti-spy technology.

"What is it, Nessie?"

"I was told to brief you." She sounded annoyed.

"Okay, I'm on my way. Can it wait?"

The woman sniffed disdainfully. "You'd have to leave immediately anyway, so I might as well tell you now."

"Okay." After a quick mirror and camera check, Daniel changed lanes.

"Most of the prisoners who escaped the other day were recaptured immediately. Didn't even make it off the grounds. That said, a small number did escape. An informant may have a line on Saram, a Light Elf assassin. He'll meet you at Lucky's."

Daniel gritted his teeth. He needed to get to headquarters, and Lucky's was in the opposite direction. "Can't this wait?"

Nessie snorted. "An ultramax in the basement of CIA headquarters is extremely foolish, but it *was* there, and dangerous men have escaped. Get to Lucky's and talk to the informant, a man named Ralph. I understand that he refuses to meet anywhere else. He's already been paid for the information, so you simply need to acquire it from him. Also, the information is time-sensitive, so no, it can't wait."

The agent snorted. The gold-toothed bottom-dweller had won the informant lotto a lot lately.

I wonder if he's hooked into something special?

Daniel sighed. "Okay, I'll head over there."

"Thank you."

Nessie ended the call.

His shoulder ached, and he wasn't even sure why. Yes, he'd been wounded in Montreal by the New Veil, but he'd not had much trouble since then, even while raiding black sites or the secret prison at headquarters.

Is this my body saying it's as annoyed as I am?

Daniel's frustration mounted as he made his way down the stairs. He should be at CIA headquarters finding out the damned truth. Why someone on a different planet had sent him a ten-year-old boy with coded messages about his mentor and mysterious plans was his first priority.

He sighed, and took a deep breath as he reminded himself not to be too upset. After all, his invasion of the prison level had resulted in Saram's escape. He was the one who had chosen to bring Paul in and not explain things well enough to avoid chaos.

It'll be a real adventure, managing the Codex team.

He looked around. Even though it was early in the day, Lucky's was full. Daniel wasn't surprised that the owner was nowhere in sight. The man liked the nightlife, but he had to sleep sometime.

Several round tables near the bar had been removed and replaced by long tables holding heated buffet trays. It'd been so long since he'd been there during the day that he'd forgotten the buffets. Lucky's was a good place for dangerous people to sample a high-quality buffet without the risk of getting shot.

Daniel blinked in disbelief at a few gnomes in rainbow-colored suits chatting around a table. The questionable fashion didn't surprise him. The presence of a certain glasses-wearing overweight pixie did. A large plastic bag floated behind her.

What the hell? Madge?

She looked his way and fluttered over. The bag trailed behind her. "Hey, Daniel," she chimed, her voice as deep as ever.

He stared at her. "Since when do you come to Lucky's?"

Madge shrugged. "All the time. Where do you think I get half the lunchroom food for the office?"

"I've never seen you here before."

She shook a finger at him. "There are many things you've never seen, but that doesn't mean they aren't real or don't happen. Humans can be so oblivious."

Daniel shook his head and ignored the bait. "How do you afford the membership?"

Madge crossed her tiny arms. "I have money, but in this case someone else is paying." She nodded toward the Rainbow Suit Brigade at the table. "Those gnomes are friends of mine. I know a lot of them, and word gets around when you're useful. It never hurts to befriend a gnome. Anyway, got to go, hon." She flew toward the door. It opened, and she disappeared up the stairs with her cargo in tow.

I bet that pixie has more of a story than any of us know.

Daniel chuckled and surveyed the bar. Ralph had again managed to find the darkest corner to skulk in. The agent headed over and sat across from him.

The informant looked up with his gold-toothed smile.

Today he wore an even nicer suit than he had the last time they had talked. "Glad you showed up so promptly. Don't let anyone ever say I'm not a man of my word. I got my money, so I want to give my info to a representative of the fine people who paid me."

Daniel ordered a Manhattan from a waitress. Even if he didn't plan to drink it, he couldn't violate Rule #2. Some fools thought they could get away with violating rules when Lucky wasn't there, but that always ended painfully —and sometimes lethally—for them.

Fortunately, the interpretations of the rules were very literal. He had to *buy* a drink, not consume one.

Once the woman had wandered off, Daniel nodded at Ralph. "Word is you have some info on Saram."

"Yep. The slice-and-dice king himself." He picked up his almost-empty glass.

"Nomad?" Daniel asked.

Ralph shook his head. "Vodka." He downed it in one gulp. "The thing is, Saram had dropped off the face of the Earth. Everyone assumed he got iced. Then, the next thing you know, he showed up yesterday and began to make trouble. He fucks with people—mostly other scum, but you know how this goes. Word is he was locked up, but someone sprung him. He has already killed two men to make a point. I think it's to establish that he's back and not to be fucked with."

"He's an assassin. It won't be long before he kills innocent people again."

The informant snorted. "Innocent? How can you say that with a straight face, Mr. Black Suit? There ain't no such thing as an innocent person on this planet or Oriceran."

Daniel shrugged. "I'm not here to debate how corrupt the world is. I want to find Saram."

Ralph smirked. "Your boy found himself a new posse already."

The pair fell silent as the waitress returned with Daniel's drink.

She handed him the glass with a smile. "Anything else, sir?"

Daniel shook his head. "No, that's all. Thank you."

Ralph stared at her ass for a long moment before focusing on his companion. "Think about that. The guy was locked up somewhere and all but gone. He gets out, and within a day, he already has a posse. Now that's a badass. You gonna go against a badass? I think the universe is trying to tell you something. Maybe you should leave well enough alone."

"It'd be nice if dangerous scum were all easy to beat, but it never seems to work that way." Daniel shrugged. "Are the guys he's hanging out with magicals?"

"Yep. A group of wizards. Real dangerous assholes. From what I hear, they're into freaky magic, and they don't mind fucking people up to make an example of them."

The CIA man frowned. "Necromancers?"

The informant shook his head. "Nah, weird stuff like twisting people up and shit, but while they're still alive. Real freaks. They get off on it."

Daniel shrugged, his expression carefully deadpan. "Weird and evil shit is a normal Monday for me."

"Just saying." Ralph pointed at the Manhattan. "You gonna drink that?"

The agent shook his head and pushed the glass over.

The informant downed the drink and hissed. "Damn, that's good." He rattled off an address. "An abandoned high school in Anacostia. That's their little playhouse for now, but word on the street is they won't be there more than a few days. Saram has a big job lined up for his new team, and after that they'll split."

Daniel stood. "I guess I need to have a little chat with them before they leave."

Ralph gave him a toothy grin. "I'd tell you good luck, but I don't really like you much."

"You don't have to give me info."

The informant snorted. "I don't like you, but I like your money."

CHAPTER EIGHTEEN

The next day, Daniel sat in the Jaguar, which was parked down the street from the abandoned high school. A further briefing with Nessie had confirmed that Saram was the elf with the X-shaped scar he'd seen during the escape.

Definitely my mess to clean up, then. Besides, the guy's an arrogant asshole and a ruthless killer. I'm so tied up in this spy-versus-spy bullshit that I sometimes forget how damned satis-fying it is to eradicate normal scum.

He'd actually turned down reinforcements. While most interpreted this as him trying to show off, Daniel couldn't risk something slipping out about his involvement in the prison escape.

Although he'd worn a chameleon mask, it was a techno-logical disguise rather than a magical one. He couldn't be sure that the elf wouldn't know he'd been there. One wrong word to a CIA agent, and Fortis would raid his place the next day and drag him and his grandfather to a black site for aggressive interrogation.

Still, he was being careful. He'd asked Nessie for extra gear, including some of the special advanced gadgets the Company didn't even have yet. This wasn't a raid against fellow CIA agents. It was a search-and-destroy mission, which gave him a wonderful freedom.

Daniel brought up the drone control app on his Company phone. He tapped through their cameras and studied the area. No one else was within several hundred yards, which made sense. Anyone who lived in a rough neighborhood quickly recognized new gangs and dangerous turf. The twisted and unnatural decorations littering the area were more than enough to reinforce the danger.

The wizards had bent and warped cars, garbage cans, shopping carts, and other items almost beyond recognition.

His face twitched as a memory of a dead man in Munich seeped in.

They don't have a molecular rearrangement gun. It's only magic, and a wizard or elf can't do much if you blow their head off.

Daniel switched to thermal images from the drone feeds. Ten signatures glowed. Six sat in one room and four in another, closer to the door. One roamed the hallways—a sentry, perhaps. He hadn't expected a whole damned nest of dangerous vermin.

I definitely need to clean this shit up.

He allowed himself a grin. The fun part of eradicating garbage and cockroaches was that the police didn't look too hard. They tended to chalk it up to gang-on-gang violence, which made it easy to cover incidents up even if he went a little over the top.

And he planned to go more than a little over the top today.

Daniel tapped a few commands on the touchscreen of his Jaguar.

The trunk popped open.

Arming sequence initiated. Linking to external targeting feed. Deploying drone swarm.

He smirked. "Consider this a field test, Nessie. Nothing says we can't mix a little rogue action and tech into normal Company missions."

Dozens of palm-sized drones whizzed out. He pressed a button, and the trunk closed.

Daniel ignored the main console. At this point, he cycled through camera feeds from the other drones. The swarm of microdrones flew low toward the school.

A dozen slammed into a window and the small amount of explosive in each ignited. The pop of impact might be mistaken for a firecracker, but a dozen of them erupting at once was more than enough to shatter the pane.

He watched the heat signatures. The drone swarm was close to the sentry and the group of four. All had reacted, but the six farther away didn't seem to have heard.

The swarm went into a farther room, and another half-dozen sacrificed themselves to make a new hole. The small explosives were bright under the thermal scan. The sentry ran around the corner, and the swarm charged him. He fell almost instantly.

A tiny amount of explosive in a shaped charge might do

little damage to a vehicle, but it was more than enough to reach a man's brain.

The rest of the swarm advanced down a hallway. The four other men rushed out of the room. The thermal scan registered several bright flashes, and the drones vanished one by one—spells of some type, the agent realized. The few remaining microdrones reached the group and introduced new holes into three of the terrorists' heads.

All microdrones feeds inactive.

Okay, Nessie. That worked out well.

The lone survivor of the four-man group rushed toward his six cohorts, who were now headed his way. Daniel had thinned the pack a little, but he still had seven magicals to deal with. He tapped a few more commands in.

"Time for Big Brother to play."

Arming sequence initiated. Arming sequence complete.

He smirked and entered a final command. All but one of the larger drones dive-bombed the school, their cameras providing a satisfying view. They slammed into the roof near the group of seven men and exploded in a huge fireball.

Daniel looked out his window at the cloud of fire and debris a half-block down.

Okay, maybe I overdid it a tad.

From the shapes he identified on the remaining drone's thermal scan, there were four enemies left. Much better odds.

He tapped in a final command, and the drone in the sky exploded. He didn't want the Company examining its footage, and Ronni and Paul had made sure that it didn't transmit remotely. He had no reason to spoil the fun of his advanced gadgets' field tests with CIA inquiries about where they had come from.

Daniel sighed. "I'd better hurry. They can only delay the police for so long."

He opened the door, stepped out of the car, and unholstered his first gun, a heavy black affair with a wide bore. The agent inserted a magazine filled with exploding rounds, and it clicked home softly.

Tempted to test the silver blast pistol tucked inside his jacket, he glanced at it briefly but resisted. He'd gauge the effect of the other weapon against the magicals first.

As he jogged down the street, he double-checked the multiple forcefield watches he wore. The defensive accessory might not work against magic, but if the enemy focused on manipulating physical objects and using them, the forcefields might save his life.

We need to make one of these that lasts more than thirty seconds, Nessie.

Daniel hurried through the smoke toward the front door and kicked it open, his explosive pistol ready. A horrible buzzing noise alerted him, and he jumped aside as a blue pulse of energy surged past him and smashed into the front door, which crunched and twisted in on itself.

"Shit." The agent fired several quick shots at the distant wizard.

The enemy leapt to the side, perhaps thinking he'd be safe if slightly wounded. His scream echoed down the hallway as the exploding bullets blew shrapnel into him. His wand clattered to the tile.

Daniel activated his first forcefield watch and a

chameleon ball. He waited a few seconds, then raced around the corner. Pipes erupted from the walls like fingers to crush him. The metal bounced off the forcefield, but the resulting flash disrupted his camouflage.

He ducked under the pipes and into a corridor as a wall exploded behind him. The blast knocked him forward, but the forcefield protected him. Unfortunately, it died a second later.

Okay, one more forcefield left.

He moved forward, tense and alert. There should only be three active enemies left.

Daniel spotted the onyx tip of the wand before the next wizard turned the corner. He whipped his gun up and squeezed a volley into the corner wall. The shower of sharp debris strafed the wizard, who yelped and dropped his wand.

The agent charged while he holstered his first weapon and yanked out his blast pistol. He leapt across the hallway, aimed at the stunned man, and pulled the trigger. A soft blue beam buzzed from Daniel's small gun and burned a hole through the target's chest, and the wizard fell back with a thud.

Another wizard stood beside Saram about ten yards back. A swirling, twisted ray blasted from the magical's wand. Daniel threw himself sideways and barely avoided a blast to the chest. His decision to not turn to shoot had saved him. He rolled to the other side of the hallway when he heard the unmistakable buzz of another discharge.

The beam hit a locker nearby. The rusted blue metal became a jiggling syrupy mass of gelatin in an instant. The substance sagged into an unrecognizable heap.

What the hell kind of wizard practices instant-gelatin magic?

Daniel thrust himself to his feet and fired instinctively. The magical shrieked as the hail of bullets released their deadly shrapnel. Daniel smiled as the man dropped, still clutching his wand.

I really, really like this gun. Nessie needs to let the Company have it.

"You think I didn't see the suit?" Saram had pulled back and now yelled from down the hallway. "You think I don't know what this is?"

Daniel snorted and didn't turn the corner. "What do you think this is?"

"Someone took the trouble to spring me from your little spook dungeon, and now you want me back there." Saram laughed. "Do you think I'm impressed? I've escaped from more prisons than you know about, human. I've even escaped from Trevilsom." He inhaled sharply. "And you want to waste the gift of freedom I was given?"

I'm the one who gave it to you. Well, Paul was, technically, but I reserve the right to take it back.

"If you want," Daniel shouted, "we can do this the easy way. You can surrender. I'll tranq you, and they can stick you back in their little ultramax. You get your three square meals a day and the occasional visit from an angry CIA agent."

"You think you're funny, don't you, human? You killed my new friends."

Wait, I'm missing something. What is it?

He wished he could turn the corner and see his target, but he wasn't sure he could take the elf out if he was close.

He looked around, but saw no mirrored surfaces that would reflect movement.

"Your friend tried to turn me into Jell-O." Daniel took a deep breath and tilted his head. Something prickled at the back of his mind.

Saram laughed. "Yeah, I know. What a bunch of freaks!"

The operative stiffened when he finally realized what it was. The echoes of the assassin's yell had been warped, as if they came from all directions.

He spun and raised his weapon. The elf stood only a few yards behind him with two iridescent knives in his hands. His scar glowed menacingly as he blurred into motion.

Daniel didn't fire, but dropped his pistol and slapped the remaining forcefield watch. Saram's blades bounced off the field, and the hazy form of the assassin cleared to reveal the smile on his face.

He only had thirty seconds before the forcefield ran out.

Twenty-eight...twenty-seven...twenty-six...

"Good instincts, human. Most people try to kill me before I reach them." Saram shook his head. "It never works."

Twenty...nineteen...eighteen...

I'm almost out of time, and this asshole will gut me the minute my forcefield drops.

Daniel whipped out the first pistol and inserted a magazine of exploding bullets. He opened fire on Saram, but the assassin's glowing blades deflected the bullets into the walls as he laughed.

Ten...nine...eight...

"I think I liked the Jell-O guy better," Daniel muttered.

Saram circled him. "You've put up a better fight than most."

Four...three...two...one...

The CIA agent jerked his gun up and fired into the ceiling. Saram hissed, distracted when the drywall and insulation showered onto him. Daniel bounded back and fired several successive shots at the elf's feet, and a final round at his chest. The assassin deflected the lower bullets with his blade, but the final slug ripped into his chest. The pop of the explosion blew a hole through him. He spun several times before collapsing on the floor.

Daniel reloaded and stepped back. There was no way he would get close.

Saram's laugh ended in a blood-filled cough. The intensity of the scar's radiance flared for several seconds before the agent had to look away. A harsh, dissonant noise was followed by a loud bang.

Daniel shook his head to clear it and looked at his adversary. Only remnants of his clothes fluttered in the air, surrounded by a pink cloud.

What the fuck was that? Self-destruct, or too much damage?

He exhaled a long, tension-filled breath.

Jell-O rays? Guys exploding into pink clouds? Okay, Ralph was right. This was weird shit.

CHAPTER NINETEEN

Daniel punched a code into his console and the garage door to Smiling Dan's lifted. The car rolled into the deep darkness, and he waited to see if anyone would appear. Given that it was the middle of the night, he didn't expect the technicians to be there, but he couldn't be sure.

The tech storage and repair warehouse for rogue CIA operations seemed nothing more than a normal garage at first glance.

Lights flicked on automatically, but no one came running.

I don't have a good explanation for why I'm here. Then again, I'm the operational head, so maybe I do.

He didn't bother with a disguise. While he knew he was recorded, if everything went well, the toys he had borrowed would be returned before Nessie even knew they were gone.

Daniel strode down a hallway. He ignored the storeroom she had shown him previously and turned a corner.

The agent had discovered his present destination purely by chance. Nessie had left a document open on a tablet at the brownstone. He assumed her guard was down because she was at the rogue office rather than CIA headquarters, and had skimmed it quickly in an automatic response. Years of CIA training and instinct prodded him to acquire useful intelligence no matter where he found it.

The document had consisted of notes to herself about her so-called Advanced Research Projects. Although written more as reminders to Nessie and a select group of Codex techs, the notes detailed a stash of even more advanced, untested, and unstable technology that she stored at Smiling Dan's.

Funny, an off-the-books research area even for a rogue operation. But I'm no better. It's not like I brought the molecular rearrangement gun here for them to examine.

He shook his head as he marched to the thick metal door marked with a rather boring title, Storage Room Three. A keypad and DNA scanner were mounted alongside.

If I try to open this door with any of the tools Nessie gave me, she'll know immediately what happened.

Daniel pressed the joker card against the door. The keypad beeped, and the door unlocked.

Okay, that's two out of five uses.

He stepped inside and flipped on the harsh overhead lighting. Rows of tables filled the large room, and metal shelves covered the back wall. Various pieces of equipment sat atop the tables, mostly in pieces.

The agent moved toward the closest table and looked down at a work in progress. Rune-covered crystals had been partially embedded in a gun, a mixture of magic and technology.

I wonder what the world will be like in two hundred years, once we really get used to all this magic?

He tore his gaze away and headed toward the shelves. The interesting technology might filter down to him eventually, but for now, he sought something in particular that Nessie had mentioned briefly in her notes. He'd need that particular toy for his next stop that night.

Daniel moved from shelf to shelf, searching for a small gray USB stick. His breathing sped up as he searched the shelves without results. Finally, he located the device tucked in a corner of the final shelf.

Just my luck.

He drew a deep breath and reached to grab the stick, but his hand hovered for a moment.

I'm crossing a line here. I could have asked her, but she's never mentioned this to me, so I'm not even supposed to know it exists.

Daniel snatched the stick from the shelf.

I'm sorry, Nessie. I need to find the truth. Tim's holding something back, something that might lead to my parents, and I've tried asking him.

He stared at the USB stick in his palm for several seconds before slipping it into his pocket.

"If no one will tell me the truth, I'll have to drag it out of them."

The elevator dinged, and Daniel stepped off and headed

down the hall toward Timothy's office. Several people tapped at computers in the cubicles nearby. There might be fewer people there than during the day, but the CIA never truly slept. It wasn't like America's enemies only operated during East Coast business hours.

Not only that, but after the Level Three-E incident, the Company had increased all-hours staffing. Part of the reason was to recapture the escapees, but it was also designed to ensure that sufficient personnel were on duty should another major escape occur.

Of course, most of the Agency now knew that there was an ultramax beneath headquarters. Few people had evinced surprise. Daniel noticed that the few terse official reports on the incident had neatly omitted any mention of aliens. Matteas and his friends were only described as "terrorists, most likely connected to New Veil and other extremist organizations."

No one now present paid the agent much attention. There was no reason to suspect anyone who walked around the upper levels in a suit with a CIA badge during extra staffing hours.

Daniel resisted a smirk. This was one of the few times that agency paranoia might work to his advantage. The more difficult part would be to gain entry without alerting anyone, but he had Ronni's camera spoofer.

From what she and Big Gnome had told him after the Level Three-E incident, the device should still work since it was partially magical. The CIA would eventually get help from the PDA and release counter-measures for the more creative toys, but insularity and compartmentalization had made the agency more vulnerable than they should be.

I wonder if they have some sort of anti-magic woven into those cells? They had plenty of magicals down there.

Daniel activated the video-feed spoofer in his pocket. It was still disguised as a G.I. Joe action figure from the early decades of the twenty-first century.

He chuckled and shook his head, wondering if Ronni was simply messing with him when she pretended not to understand some of his references.

Then again, it's all been kids' toys. Maybe she doesn't know about anything that's not related to kids' stuff.

Daniel waited a few seconds and stepped toward Timothy's door. He looked around, and the hallway was empty. Confident that the cameras would show nothing, he pulled out the joker.

His mentor was paranoid enough that he'd figure out someone had broken into his office if he used conventional methods, but even Timothy had probably not planned for a magical card.

Taking a deep breath, the agent placed the card against the door. The lock clicked open.

That's three times. Only two left. Funny how often I'm using it.

He opened the door, stepped inside, and closed it behind him.

Daniel hurried over to the computer and sat down. He slipped some gloves on and moved the mouse. The screen came to life, but the device was locked.

Yeah, I didn't think it'd be that easy.

He plugged in the gray USB stick he'd taken from Nessie's stash, and it hummed softly.

I hope that means it's working.

The screen flashed a few times, and the desktop appeared. A box popped up with a prompt.

Aladdin Advanced Intrusion Tools 2.241a. Enter query:

Daniel typed "Belize" and hit enter. An hourglass appeared, and he gritted his teeth. He glanced intermittently at the door as if he expected his mentor to walk in any second and demand to know what he was doing.

I guess I could demand the same of him. The question is whether he'd tell the truth, and if I would know if he did. The guy's lied for a living since I was a kid. Hell, he taught me how to lie better.

The computer beeped.

One result found.

A window popped up with a hidden folder.

Daniel clicked to open it and found a single text document named BELIZE.

Now, what do we have here? You've kept secrets from me, Tim.

He opened the file. Three pairs of coordinates at the top of the document were labeled LAT and LONG.

The agent entered the first pair of coordinates into his phone. They brought up a rural area of western China. The next set showed a destination deep in the jungles of Brazil. The final pair marked a hilly but non-developed area in the Faroe Islands. The South American coordinates were the closest to Belize, and they were still over three thousand miles away.

He frowned as he considered what the coordinates meant. As far as he could tell from satellite images, the areas marked were all in the middle of nowhere. They were also rural and undeveloped, with little evidence of anyone living nearby.

Why does he care about random spots in random countries?

Daniel scrolled down. His eyes widened, and his heart rate kicked up as he read the classified document.

Recovered from the remains of the journal of Brian Winters near the site of interest AJ42-345.

The journal entry was dated the day before his parents were reported missing, and the beginning was nothing but gibberish. The recovered entry had more missing letters and words than text.

...realize now...were wrong. We thought we knew what the Codex of the Sky Gods meant and understood the nature of the gateway...the key is the town.

...unsure if they're dangerous. The alien technology is well beyond anything our species will be capable of for centuries, and it's clearly not magical. We were able to discuss with...

Temporal displacement and access don't seem to be limited to their kind. The lack of magic associated with it probably explains why no one has been able to track them down before. Still...

...can be reasoned with...

...know all the risks...shouldn't be fatal. They better understand it now.

They...we should be back soon.

The entry ended. The last line in the file was obviously from whoever had prepared the document.

Additional physical reproduction failed. Advanced algorithmic reconstruction failed.

Daniel stared at the screen for several minutes. Even with all the missing text, the journal entry clearly suggested his parents had found the site they had searched for, and had perhaps even established contact with the aliens.

Temporal displacement was consistent with what he'd observed from the returnees, who had all been taken at different times. The question of why this was happening and what the aliens' goals were remained unanswered.

Daniel frowned as he noticed the date the document had been prepared, which was several years after his parents' disappearance but well before he'd joined the CIA. If Tim had access to this document years before, he would have known that the couple might have been involved in alien research. He should have told Daniel about it immediately.

On the other hand, maybe the man had just received the document. That aside, he still hadn't bothered to hand it over or inform his mentee.

The agent breathed deeply to calm himself. He pulled the device from the computer, which relocked itself immediately.

Daniel shook his head. Both his grandfather and his mentor were keeping things from him.

Who the hell can I trust?

Daniel sighed as he used the joker to unlock the door to Storage Room Three.

That's four. One more use.

The door clicked open, and after flipping the lights on, he replaced the intrusion stick where he'd found it. He hated having to go behind Nessie's back like that, but normal hacking wouldn't have sufficed. Daniel couldn't have asked Ronni or Paul to help him access the protected system of a paranoid CIA senior agent.

With one last glance, he left the room and the lock clicked behind him. As he walked toward the main garage, a shadow moved at the edge of the hallway. He wasn't alone.

The agent paused and drew his gun. He'd thought he'd been careful at headquarters, but maybe someone had seen him break into Timothy's office and decided to follow him.

He crept forward as the shadow stretched across the hallway. Someone was coming around the corner. He raised his gun and blinked as Nessie appeared and eyed him balefully.

"I'd appreciate it if you didn't shoot me, Daniel." She snorted and folded her arms. "And after you broke into my supply room, too. Talk about rude!"

Daniel holstered his gun and rubbed the back of his neck. "You knew?"

"Nothing leaves that room without a notification coming to me." She fixed him with a withering look. "I applaud you for getting through the lock without it informing me, though. You're even more resourceful than I imagined, but that doesn't alter the fact that you'd better have a damned good reason for what you've done."

He shrugged. "Well, you see, I needed access to a place that I couldn't gain entry to without special toys."

Nessie narrowed her eyes. "And this place required you to steal devices from me?"

"'Steal' is a very strong word." Daniel nodded toward the storage room. "I brought it back, so it's more like 'borrowed.'" He forced a grin. "And for once, I didn't break anything and everything worked exactly as it should. That has to be worth something, right?"

She snorted again and pinched the bridge of her nose. "Don't embarrass yourself. The worst part is that had you simply asked me, I would have agreed. I thought I'd already shown you where my loyalties lie."

He nodded. "I'm sorry, but I had my reasons."

"Don't we all?" Nessie marched past him to the storage room. She entered the code and put her thumb on the DNA scanner. "We'll never succeed if we can't trust each other, Daniel." She stepped in and slammed the door shut.

He continued toward the car. Nessie was right, but that was the problem. Men he should have been able to trust—like Timothy or his grandfather—had kept important information from him.

"We'll soon see who I *can* trust."

CHAPTER TWENTY

Daniel strolled into the operations room to find Ronni peering at a stretchy orange octopus toy. She soldered a circuit inside, and wisps of smoke rose into the air. He sniffed a few times. It smelled like incense.

"Hey, Ronni. Why aren't you in your little work area?"

She shrugged. "More people walk through here, sir. The problem is that without a lot of team members, it gets weird and quiet. At least, it does when Madge isn't here, and she's off running errands."

Daniel chuckled and leaned over the table with his phone out. "I wondered if you would do me a quick favor. I need you to check on something."

Ronni set her tools down and pulled a keyboard over. "What did you need?"

"I want a recent satellite image of the following coordinates." He rattled off the China set.

A few seconds later, the globe display transformed into a flat image. Nothing but scrubland and light desert stretched for miles.

"I have two more to check."

Ronni nodded.

The next images weren't any more impressive. All were identical to what he'd found when he'd checked the available commercial imagery. There was nothing even vaguely noteworthy about the coordinates other than that all three were in wilderness areas far from cities.

Daniel frowned. "Damn."

She looked curiously at him. "What's wrong?"

He shook his head. "Nothing. I'm following up on something."

Jake ran into the room with a grin, his wooden breakdancing toy in hand. "Daniel."

The operative smiled at the boy, almost jealous of his innocence.

"Hey, Jake. How about we get you something special to eat?"

<hr>

The quick morning trip had been a plan to hopefully jog a few memories. Daniel reasoned that the boy must be American, given his accent. Since he hadn't seemed astonished at the existence of electronics, he'd likely been taken in the last century. If so, he might recognize McDonald's. The agent smiled as the boy all but inhaled his French fries.

"These are great. Super-great." Jake beamed.

The other returnees clearly remembered where they came from, but weren't able to recall much of what had happened after their abduction. The boy seemed to be the opposite, and Daniel wondered if the difference in memory retention was age-related.

If that was the case, the boy could potentially help him with clues that might lead him to his parents.

The key is the town.

That part of his father's journal entry stuck out in Daniel's mind. Had he referred to the missing village? Something had happened there. After what Daniel had seen in Baja and when Matteas departed, he could easily imagine a small village destroyed in the process of opening an alien portal.

He had many clues now, but they only pointed at aliens. While he wasn't sure how many potential aliens had been recaptured, he couldn't risk another trip to Hangar Twelve anytime soon—especially with the agency's current critical-alert level. For all he knew, they'd been moved to a new location.

Daniel leaned in with a warm smile. "Did you come to these kinds of places before you were taken?"

The boy shrugged. "I don't know. I don't remember. I don't remember a lot about over there either, but I don't think we had French fries." He popped another fry into his mouth.

"I'm less interested in wherever they took you than where they took you from. Do you remember who the president was?"

Jake shook his head.

"Maybe what the popular movies were?"

He received another shake of the head and a shrug this time. "I was really little, so I don't remember much at all. Sorry."

Daniel kept the smile on his face. There was no point harassing a child who clearly didn't have much to offer. He'd have to give the boy time and hope he eventually remembered.

Jake pulled the small toy from his Happy Meal box, a VTOL plane. He made engine sounds and pretended it was flying.

He's only a kid. I don't know why they took him, but at least they didn't hurt any of them.

Daniel blinked at the thought. The returnees might not remember much, but they were all in good health and had no signs of major injury. Chen bore a few scars, but he'd explained that he'd received them before he left. Kevin had a similar story.

After the torture that woman received at headquarters, they could have screwed me over. They could have shown up with a molecular rearrangement gun and turned me into Jell-O like those wizards tried to, but they didn't. They showed more humanity than Troy and his buddies.

The boy gobbled his meal, clutching his toy plane with his free hand.

The aliens might be dangerous, but if the boy was any indication, they weren't evil.

The agent would have to solve what mysteries he could and wait for more information on the aliens. He'd learned more about his mentor, but he still felt that his grandfather was hiding something from him. At least that situation didn't require advanced gadgets.

It's time to drop the kid off and force Pops to tell me everything he knows.

Later that night, Jake pulled his blanket over his head. The beds were comfortable enough in the brownstone, and he had no complaints.

He withdrew what looked like a marker from his pocket and rubbed the side. It shimmered, and revealed a metallic silver-green rod with two grooves. His communicator.

The boy squeezed the grooves on the side, and the rod twisted and lit up. He tilted his head to read the symbols as they appeared in the air.

They wanted a status report.

He pressed the grooves again and lifted the communicator for a brief response. *"I'm in."*

Daniel lingered near the back room in the shop, watching as his grandfather finished with a customer.

The smiling man pulled a cloth-wrapped wooden tennis racquet out of a paper bag on the counter. He turned and swung it several times. "I can't believe how much this will improve my game."

Peter sighed. "It's self-stringing—that's it. There's no magic in there that will improve your game. I don't want you to buy it under false pretenses."

The customer grinned. "You say that, but you can't be sure."

The older man shrugged. "No, I can't."

"Don't worry. I only have myself to blame if this doesn't

turn out as I want." He lowered the racquet, re-wrapped it in the cloth, and slipped it into the bag again.

"Do you want a paper receipt, or is electronic fine?"

"Electronic."

Peter nodded. "Then we're all done here. Thanks for stopping by."

He glanced at Daniel, who gave him a somber look before heading into the back room. The agent sat at the table and activated his silence cube.

No more waiting. It was time someone told him the truth. He deserved it.

His grandfather walked in and frowned. "What's wrong with you? You look like a man condemned to suck down nothing but mud for his next three meals." His gaze dipped to the silence cube. "And why do you need that thing?"

Daniel shrugged. "I'm interested in the truth, and don't want the wrong people to overhear."

"The truth?"

"Yes." He frowned. "Let's start with a simple question. Who are you?"

His grandfather snorted. "The last time I checked, I was Peter Rooney."

Daniel shook his head. "But who are you *really*?"

"What are you going on about? I'm your grandfather. I was in the Army, then I opened this shop." The old man shrugged. "I was married to a wonderful woman who died too soon and I've been too lazy to leave this neighborhood, but I can't complain too much. Unlike a lot of neighborhoods, it hasn't gone downhill."

His grandson stared at him, his lips pursed. "You know

I lie for a living, and that's without all the other secrets I have to keep."

Peter shook his head. "You know my secrets. I showed you the vault, after all. What is this about? I'm the one who should complain. You give my Fresca away all the time, and you don't always replace it."

Daniel narrowed his eyes. "I'm not joking, Pops. If you want me to trust you, it's time you leveled with me. You know something about aliens—a lot more than what was in my parents' journals."

His grandfather crossed his arms, his expression bland. "And why do you think that?"

The agent slammed his palm on the table, and the cube shook. "Because a damned alien the CIA had locked up told me to talk to you. An alien who I had to help to escape the agency. Stop playing stupid, Pops. It's a fucking insult to us both. I've told you the truth. You know about me being in the CIA, and you know about my side job looking into aliens."

The old man sighed heavily and uncrossed his arms, then turned and headed into the main shop. He locked the front door and flipped the store sign to CLOSED before returning to the back room.

The old man dropped into a chair across from his grandson. "You have to understand that I was trying to protect you."

Daniel snorted. "Protect me? How can you say that after all that's happened?"

Peter averted his gaze. "Yes, protect you. This alien stuff is dangerous—very dangerous. Even with your CIA work, this is a whole different level of dangerous."

"How do you even know about any of this?" Daniel glanced at the door leading to the basement. "From my parents?"

His grandfather shook his head. "When I was in Afghanistan with the Army, I saw something. Strange lights. When I reported them I thought they would laugh, but instead, I was immediately transferred to a unit that helped the government investigate alien stuff." He shrugged. "I had a few—whatever you want to call it—close encounters. Nothing big, but enough to realize something."

Daniel nodded. "Now we're getting somewhere. Hopefully, closer to the truth. What did you realize?"

"The aliens are a lot like us."

"What? You mean humanoid?"

Peter shook his head. "No, I mean they aren't angels or demons. They're a mixed bag. Some are assholes, some aren't, but they're definitely not all bad."

The agent pushed his impatience aside. "And the *Codex of the Sky Gods*? Are you the one who pushed Mom and Dad to look into it?"

"No, not at all. At first, I discouraged them. I believed it was something that they shouldn't poke their noses into, but it's not like they listened to me." Peter exhaled a wistful sigh. "Your parents found out more in a few years of serious investigation than I did in my entire time in the Army."

His grandson frowned. "Why didn't you tell me all this before?"

"I didn't know what to say. I...wanted you to know about how your parents might have disappeared, but I was also worried that you'd become obsessed and make the same mistake they did." Peter snorted. "But now you're knee-deep in it, so I guess there was no point in hiding it." He looked down at the table, a distant expression on his face. "You talked about lying all the time, so you know how it is. After years of pretending to be something or not be something, you simply get used to it. It's hard to break free."

Daniel sucked in a breath. "Did they know about you? That you looked into this in the Army?"

He nodded. "A little. A lot of it was highly classified, and I was always scared that if I said too much some asshole in a black suit would show up and take me away."

The agent snorted. "I guess I can't say you're wrong there." He stilled. "Wait, did you know Tim?"

Peter shook his head. "If I met him, I didn't know it."

"He's been on this shit for a while. The way he's acted, I'm convinced he knows about you. He probably came across your name in reports." Daniel frowned and looked down. "Not that he bothered to tell me."

The old man chuckled. "I know I'm a little older, but sometimes you have to give us old farts a break. We get stuck in our ways."

"Maybe." Daniel needed more. "And you're sure you were dealing with aliens back in the day? I mean, actual non-Oriceran extraterrestrials? Most of your time in the Army was before the truth about Oriceran came out."

Peter shrugged. "It was hard to investigate weird stuff without running across an Oriceran or two, but when the Paranormal Defense chaps got involved, we were able to figure out this wasn't the same thing. Besides, the aliens use a lot of tech. That was an easy tell." He laughed.

"Somehow finding out about magic didn't bother me as much as the aliens, maybe because of all the crazy tech. The weird magic didn't bother me as much as the strange devices. Stuff like that gun."

Daniel snorted. "By the way, we have two of them in the vault now."

Peter almost jumped out of his seat. "What? Since when? Did it clone?"

"No, I brought the second one in after a little side job in Michigan. I looked into an alien sighting and found another gun and a communications device, which my team is looking into." He shrugged.

His grandfather heaved a huge sigh. "Since I'm being honest, there's something else I should admit."

Daniel laughed. "If you say you're not actually my grandfather, I swear I'll shoot you right now."

Peter looked up, and some of his feistiness returned via a scowl. "I'm damn well your grandfather, Daniel." His expression softened. "The elf who warned me about the gun… Well, I gave him a part, a control rod. I made a copy and put it in the gun so you wouldn't know."

"You already told me that, remember? And of all the things you've done, that bothers me the least."

"Why is that?"

Daniel nodded toward the basement door. "Because those things are dangerous. I half-wonder if I shouldn't yank this control rod from the second gun and throw it in the Potomac." He frowned. "You said you think they're a mixed bag? The aliens, that is."

"Yeah. What about it?"

"I keep finding very dangerous weapons." Daniel

shrugged. "It's like Japanese tourists showing up at the airport with rocket launchers, which makes it kind of hard to think they're purely for defensive purposes."

Peter scratched his eyebrow. "Between Oriceran and us, this planet's got nukes, magic, and scary-ass monsters. Maybe they're for emergency use in case we turn hostile."

Daniel's brow lifted. "That's not good."

"Why?"

"Most people's default state is hostile, especially to outsiders." He shook his head.

Peter glanced at one of the comic book racks and stared at an issue of *Green Lantern*. It depicted a half-dozen Green Lanterns of different species all flying in formation. "Look, it's not like they recently started visiting. If they were pissed enough to want a war, we'd probably already have it. I'm sure they have different factions or groups. Maybe it's about connecting with the right ones while there's still time."

Daniel considered that and remembered how Matteas could have killed him. It made him think a little more deeply. If he'd been held in a foreign prison and seen his friends die or be tortured, would he be willing to forgive someone working for those same people? He wasn't so sure he could, but the alien had—unless that was an act, which was possible. He shrugged off the questions this immediately raised about Matteas' possible motives.

"Okay, then. That brings me back to my parents. Everything I've found shows they're connected to aliens, and it has something to do with a missing city." Daniel drummed his fingers on the tabletop. "John Rainer guarded a guy for a while back in World War Two. This scientist was looking into a city that might have teleported. I have a hard time believing that's not related."

Peter exhaled and shook his head. "You already know much more about this kind of thing than I knew during most of my time looking into it."

"What about my parents? What do we do?"

His grandfather shrugged. "What we've been doing. We keep looking for clues."

The End

What do you get when you mix an Oriceran artifact, a little technology and a cow? Find out when Daniel returns in <u>Artifact of the True Patriot</u>.

AUTHOR NOTES - MARTHA CARR

OCTOBER 14, 2018

I am the youngest of four girls, with one younger brother. (I once heard him tell someone he had five mothers. I have no idea why...) My oldest sister, Diana is ten years older than I am and went away to boarding school when I was just two years old. My memories of her are during school breaks at Christmas time or during the summer.

She was infinitely clever and curious about everything. An older version of me but with more focus. She created our costumes for the 4th of July parade the town had every year and we'd often win. One year I was the Declaration of Independence and she burned the edges to make it look older. My sister, Cary was the Washington Monument and had to look out the two little windows at the top and follow the yellow line down the middle of the street.

If she wasn't creating costumes, she was cooking cherries jubilee and setting it on fire, or baked Alaska for my parents' bridge club night. Or she was embroidering something colorful and delicate like the vines and birds she carefully stitched down the long sides of a red cape.

On top of that she knew from an early age she wanted to be a doctor in an era (the 1960's) when women didn't normally aspire to those heights. She was determined and pursued it like it was fact.

I was watching her every move and to me she was full of magic and promise and set a good example for me. Apparently, all those naysayers were wrong. Anything is possible if you just keep going.

Eventually, she became an orthopaedic surgeon specializing in the delicate repair of hands. Fourth woman in the country to become an orthepod and the first in Virginia and had to fight her way there.

We're older now and she's not doing well. Last week I went to see her and all I could think of was when I was very small, and she was this teenager full of promise. She had the most beautiful red hair that has turned into an amazing shade of auburn.

In a moment, a lifetime goes by and the end becomes more visible than the beginning.

What makes it bearable or even a celebration is whether or not the human being who got this body for a while in order to spend some time here, did it pursuing what they wanted to be while being a part of their community. That's pretty much the entire secret of life. Loving cooperation and making sure you're having fun.

I forget that last part sometimes but fortunately, my tribe is the sort who reminds me and even laughs at my frustration, so I quickly reset back to not being the center of the universe. That helps.

To all those who paved the way, and continue to do it, so that I can have a voice and make choices and have fun, I can repay them by stretching out to fulfill those dreams. That takes courage and trust and yeah, that group of people again. I won't waste this gift and I'll go one better and do what I can to help the next ones coming up – my replacements and maybe they will have an even easier time of it – men and women of every sort – and do amazing things that make their little siblings look up and just wonder at the magnificence of the world. May you all know boundless joy in your life and love in your community with opportunities to spread your wings ever wider. More adventures to follow.

Martha

AUTHOR NOTES - MICHAEL ANDERLE

NOVEMBER 12, 2018

THANK YOU for not only reading this story but these *Author Notes* as well .

(I think I've been good with always opening with thank you. If not, I need to edit the other author notes!)

RANDOM (*sometimes*) THOUGHTS?

Right now, LMBPN Publishing (this company) is working to change Publishing. Not because we want to change the industry exactly, but rather we want to publish our way, and our way isn't working the same way as tradi-tional publishing does.

Why?

Glad you asked.

During the Great Depression (almost a hundred years ago) book stores told publishers that they wouldn't purchase books if they couldn't return them. Publishers agreed, and we STILL have a system which allows book-stores to send back non-sellers.

You might might thought they would have changed the rules once the Great Depression was over, but they didn't.

Oh, a book store can accept books for non-return (and get a larger discount) but most don't. For a smaller fiction publisher like myself here in America, it doesn't PAY to try to work this system. With digital publishing, we either get paid or we don't. Amazon allows customers to return the e-books for refunds, and some do.

However, there isn't a large percentage who return the books. When they do, we aren't out money like with paper books. If we have books we get printed for $3.00 returned to the wholesaler, then we are out that money. So, If I were to print 1,000 copies I'm out $3,000 plus shipping, storage and other costs associated with paper sales, including a percentage held back for this purpose.

There isn't much margin in paper until you charge a lot of money for it. Thus, the high paper costs.

Amazon takes a 30% cut of e-book sales (from what I understand, they reduced the cut from close to 65% due to Apple entering the market). It costs me the same amount to sell one book as it does to sell a thousand. There are no up-front costs.

For paper, we handle this by POD (Print On Demand.) The quality is there now, and we don't have to print and warehouse a thousand books.

But then, we also get charged a LARGE amount for the books to be POD. So, paper is a bad business compared to ebook.

So why do it?

Because you, the readers, want them. It usually costs about $100.00 (including overhead) to get a print-ready file, and the modifications to the cover to make a full package. We are charged for an ISBN code (anywhere from $1 in quantity to a $100 for one. It's a racket.)

So, all in, it probably costs on average (if you hire out services – which you don't have to) between $50 and $200 for most print versions to go online with POD.

We will probably recoup that investment in a year or two, unless for some reason the book sells really well. The main reason it takes that long is we sell pretty close to three hundred ebooks for every one paperback, since we don't sell through book stores.

(See comments above about why bookstore sales are challenging.)

I've spent a lot of hours trying to figure out how to hack this sales method. I KNOW it can be done, and be profitable. The challenge is that LMBPN focuses on new stories, not the infrastructure to handle paper at a larger volume. At some point, I'm hoping a knowledge fairy flies around my head and taps me, providing me with a way to make this work.

The paper business is (I think) around $4 Billion a year. I'm fine accepting even a small percentage of that, but breaking into the business cost effectively is proving challenging with so many other moving parts.

And so many holdovers from the Great Depression (plus I imagine other aspects I'm totally unfamiliar with, not having been a part of the system.)

Either way, POD (for us) is what we are staying with until I can see a way to enter the book market effectively and with less risk.

What's funny, is I'm totally willing to do the first two or three books at no profit for Indie Book Stores. Hell, I'll GIVE them the first five books of *Death Becomes Her* free if we can figure out a way to do that effectively because I believe it will spur requests for book 02 and so on. Unfortunately, there is little bookshelf space for another set of books in the stores.

HOW TO MARKET FOR BOOKS YOU LOVE

We are able to support our efforts with you reading our books and we appreciate you doing this!

If you enjoyed this or ANY book by any author, especially Indie published, we always appreciate it if you make the time to review a book, since it lets other readers who might be on the fence take a chance on it as well.

AROUND THE WORLD IN 80 DAYS

Last week, we had the 20Booksto50k Vegas conference for Indie writers. On Thursday morning, I was on an Urban Fantasy panel which Martha Carr hosted. There were FIVE of us on the panel, I sat on the seat on the left (according to those in the audience.)

Martha was standing next to me.

Now, being on a panel can be fun, but for me it can be stressful. Why? Well, when the questions hit, I like to ponder the answer, listening to the other panelists' answers before I have to provide mine.

You get more time, but occasionally someone else provides

the perfect answer, and you have to just say "what she said" or something similar.

However, we get question one…. "ANDERLE?"

I eye Martha and answer the question.

Question 2… "ANDERLE?"

I eye Martha and answer the question.

Question 3… "ANDERLE?"

I eye Martha, roll my eyes, and answer the question.

Question 4… "ANDERLE?" … the snickers are out there in the Audience when Carr admits she just likes to yell, "ANDERLE!"

I eye Martha, roll my eyes, bitch a little, and answer the question.

Question 5… "ANDERLE?"

"DAMMIT, CARR!" I yelled amid general laughter…

Question 6… "Shall we start with Jamie Davis on the other side?"

Yes, I thought. Yes we shall.

I now have a very mild form of PTSD from that session. Someone later in the day yelled "ANDERLE!" and my response (looking around) was "DAMMIT, CARR!"

FAN PRICING

If you would like to find out what LMBPN is doing and what books we will be publishing, just sign up at http://lmbpn.com/email/ . When you sign up, we notify you of the books coming out for the week, any new posts of interest in the books and pop culture arena, and the fan pricing on Saturday.

Ad Aeternitatem,

Michael Anderle

Other series in the Oriceran Universe:
THE DANIEL CODEX SERIES
I FEAR NO EVIL
THE UNBELIEVABLE MR. BROWNSTONE
SCHOOL OF NECESSARY MAGIC
THE LEIRA CHRONICLES
REWRITING JUSTICE
THE KACY CHRONICLES
MIDWEST MAGIC CHRONICLES
SOUL STONE MAGE
THE FAIRHAVEN CHRONICLES

OTHER BOOKS BY JUDITH BERENS

OTHER BOOKS BY MARTHA CARR